T0066888

SEA DIAMOND

Carey Maytham

Order this book online at www.trafford.com
or email orders@trafford.com

Most Trafford titles are also available at major online book retailers.

Printed in the United States of America.

ISBN: 978-1-4907-1581-0 (sc)
ISBN: 978-1-4907-1582-7 (e)

Trafford rev. 09/26/2013

www.trafford.com

North America & international
toll-free: 1 888 232 4444 (USA & Canada)
fax: 812 355 4082

CHAPTER 1

A fine looking elderly man sat on a comfortable armchair in a drawing room filled with antiques. His hair was white, long and wispy indicating that care was necessary. His clothes were slightly rumpled at the end of a day. There was a drizzle outside and the wind whined gently outside around the corners of the Great House in Devon. He looked wizened perhaps anxious but on the whole relaxed for his age. At the time this was owing to a brandy glass of tawny amber liquid that it was clear that he was partaking of.

This was no wonder because he had in the last few weeks experienced the death of his long term marriage partner, his much loved wife Alice. He grimaced at this reality, of the contact with the undertaker and the little church service with a few close friends in attention. A look of shock came over his face again and again as he put down the brandy glass that he noticed was contained in a shining glass polished up by his kitchen menials.

He had a few sips more and then picked up a rose tinted glass box encoated with filigreed silver. This was where he had placed his late wife's large diamond ring cared for her over their long years as man and wife. The glass box had a velvet lining and opened to a false bottom with a latch that he pressed. He looked inside expecting bitterly to see the ring there. All he could see at first was the gold circle of the diamond's clasp. His heart thumped.

Where was the dress diamond? He shook at the box impatiently. Was this a trick that the brandy was playing on him? The box rattled with the sound of two items in it. His worsening eyesight was affecting this. The diamond must be there, it surely must. Could it have come loose? As he moved the box again tilting it a little the diamond sparkled once again in his sight.

It had come loose in the urgency of the death of his wife and its aftermath. He chided himself for his carelessness. It could have been lost forever. He clipped the box closed and sat back a little taking a few more sips of the brandy. The diamond must go to Tasha his daughter. All that had happened meant that he would have to change his will. The document lay to one side on the stinkwood occasional table in front of him. He knew that he was aging now and might possibly have to be admitted to a rest home very soon.

The old man pulled towards him a cedar wood cigar box. This was an indulgence that allowed himself once in a while. As he did so he ruffled through some yellowed papers lying on the table before him. On them was printed his last will and testament that he had received from his solicitors a couple of days ago. He frowned at the effort he was having to make to peruse his instructions in this mellow situation that he had created for himself.

Since Alice his wife had died within the last few months he had to change everything in the will. Now Tasha his daughter would inherit and as a last resort in the event of her predeceasing her son out in Africa, to that young whippersnapper Jonathan his grandson. He coughed slightly as the cigar smoke caught at his throat.

A blue glow from a corner lamp stand fell soothingly onto the scene and he again looked up at the rather cluttered bric-a-brac antiques on the mantelpiece where there was a log fire underneath burning brightly. His eyes moved to the little lace covered occasional tables that his late wife had loved so much that he had indulged her in. She had virtually had an obsession for collecting antique items fully under the impression that one day they would sell for a fortune.

Old man Grant grunted cynically to himself. Of course they were worthless a female cantankerousness and illusion of Alice's but during her last months weeks and hours it was the one ploy he had used to humor her Of course now when his doctor insisted that he go into a rest home it would all have to go into a museum. The three little brass monkeys, see no evil, speak no evil, hear no evil. The collection of antique silver that she had bought for a song that one day about ten years ago and brought home so happily and pleased with herself And again looking around, that was not all he could see.

Her persian cat lay on the setee opposite and the old Afgan hound lay splayed out in front of the cosy log fire. Just as he was going to take another gulp of brandy to see himself through satisfying his conscious in reading through his will there was a knock at the door. It was his manservant. The door opened and a sleek looking menial put his head around it.

Grant snapped at him irritated by the intrusion now he was trying to concentrate. He had just got into the mood of approving and signing the will. He would wait now. Perhaps one of the other lackeys could be called in and the two of them could witness for him while he signed his last will and testament. It was uncomfortably chill that evening and neither of the two men wanted to speak. It was becoming late and gruffly Grant said:

"James is the other manservant on duty? If he is please summon him. I have a document here that needs endorsement." His man replied: "Right away sir."

Then Grant sat down again and toyed with the brandy in the shining glass. A decanter stood close to the glass. Yes he thought. Tasha, Alice had confided in him before she had died had told her mother that on a diplomatic visit to South Africa that she and her husband had met some charming people who had quite taken her fancy especially as they had a beautiful and clever daughter.

These people Alice had told Grant were apparently of recent Dutch descent in South Africa. Alice had told her husband that she would do everything possible to put Jonathan in touch with them when he had finished his mining studies in Scotland and his marine mining occupation in Sierre Leone. Jonathon would later be posted to a diamond mining barge off the coast of Namibia every two months or so, near to the estuary of the Orange River. He would have shore leave every break in the ongoing working situation.

Alice had confided in her husband that she was going to manipulate Jonathan into a relationship with Marijke these new acquaintances' daughter. Grant thought, Alice was a canny one. He took another sizeable sip of brandy as he heard the voices of the menservants approaching as he had asked. He rattled the silver filigreed glass snuff box again impatient now to get the business of the evening done and climb into a warm bed. The two lackeys entered. Grant nodded surlily though communicatively to them. One of the servants said, too inquisistively for his station in life, Grant thought: these menials were constantly over familiar at the wrong times. The man had asked:

"Will we have to peruse the document sir?" Grant snapped back irritably as the brandy took its effect. "Only two signatures of witnesses as well as mine are necessary".

The scenario had been disturbed by their entrance even though the men servants were necessary. The Afghan hound moaned complainingly in front of the fire at their intrusion and stretched. The Persian cat that had been Alice's darling sat up and began licking itself. Everyone was tired. Grand said tersely:

"Here. Sign here, first you," he indicated the nearest man, "and then you James."

Soon the document was completed and ready for Grant to deliver to the solicitor the next morning. One of the servants slipped out silently while the other raked what was left of the coals into the fireplace into ashes so he could shut up the living room for the night.

He saw that Grant had nearly finished the brandy so the other said:

"Will you be turning in now sir?" Grant was an old man, so answered crossly with the tensing but relaxing drink. He said:

"Just give me a few minutes more." "Right sir," the valet responded.

As his valet had entered the room looking impatient to shut down the living quarters for the night, Grant gave the rose glass snuff box a final rattle, closed it and put it down firmly on the polished wooden table. He addressed the valet who was clearly trying to control his irritation with the tardiness and self-indulgence of the old man who spoke in a slurred voice:

"See that nothing that I have left in here is disturbed my man. I will need these items when I see my lawyer tomorrow morning."

Tired but still looking inquisitive the valet walked over to take Grant's arm. He was clearly incapable of climbing the stairway and getting to bed on his own. Then once bedded down Grant gave a final sigh of sleep overtaking him for the night. With his brandy-ridden drowsiness in his thinking he called up the memory of Alice his wife and Tasha their daughter.

His grandson was just a faint thought coming to mind now and again as sleep overtook him. Alice! She had become more and more nervously incapable as their marriage had increased in years. She had a bad effect on Tasha in his opinion as the girl was growing up. He grunted as the first snores of the night overtook; him.

Of course Alice had always had the last word. Tasha, yes had inherited Alice's sense of being out of touch with reality and unreasonableness, including a complete disregard for the value of what money could do for one in life. She had married wealth so had never had to worry about where the next meal was coming from. And Tasha had passed onto Jonathan this complete lack of co-operation.

Jonathan was intelligent yes but had been quite obstreperous in his youth. Just like his father that pilot fellow that Tasha had involved herself with, Jonathon's father. Quite out of his mind to go and fight the war in aeroplanes that took off and landed from aircraft carrier ships. The whole situation had nearly driven them all mad.

Grant gave another grunt of satisfaction. It would have pleased Alice yes, to know that Tasha, and ultimately in the event of her predeceasing himself and his grandson, would be the heiress to the Great House. Perhaps she could get some medical help. There was a new and up and coming science, he had read in his daily newspaper, to do with the manipulation of the brain by trained specialist doctors. No, he must sleep now. He must see the lawyer in the morning. Silence fell in the bedroom and the whole house.

Grand blearily opened his eyes the next morning. He heard the faint founds of birds twittering outside. What was so urgent today? Oh! That was it. He had to see his lawyer about his will. Everything though had seemed so rosy the last evening. Now he had to face the sour faced Mr. Eggleston the solicitor. He had one or two appointments with the man and had managed to apprise him of the fact that Alice had been quite impossible. Yes. Impossible.

Now Tasha would have to be considered in the inheritance. He shaved, dressed and then found himself quite spritely in the walk down to the village where Mr. Eggleston had his rooms. He sat down and waited in the outer quarters He heard a cough and then the bent rather mean faced Mr. Eggleston made his appearance rubbing his hands together.

This man Mr. Grant Godiver, the solicitor thought to himself was wasting his time and money on all these unnecessary confidentialities and appointments with him. Still, the lawyer thought shrewdly it lined his own pocket. As usual Mr. Eggleston was not busy in this quiet market village, but yes, he did like to go into all disagreements and issues quite thoroughly for his own satisfaction. So he took the step of saying the first words as he came out of his in the meeting. His voice was sharp and clearly not intending to give way on any matter he involved himself in.

"Good day Mr. Godiver. As usual it is good to see you."

Grant had been relaxing his mind staring out of the window and had not heard Mr Eggleston's first verbal approach. He jumped up as he heard the greeting and extended a hand of greeting:

"Of course! Of course! May I have a seat in your office?" Mr. Eggleston acquiesced at this request. The two men sat down. The solicitor spoke after ruffling some papers on his desk.

"Yes I have your particulars on file. I know exactly where we have reached in our discussion about your last will and testament. To hasten this concern I think we must both realize that the heir will ultimately be you grandson Jonathan." Grant answered:

"Yes Yes, Mr. Eggleston. But I would like you to realize that he too is mentally incapable of handling such a grand inheritance." Mr. Eggleston answered:

"Your wife Alice's unrealistic and unreasonable attitude towards everything in the matter shows that she had absolutely no sense of the value of money in everything you had given her. This is a prime factor in this will we are trying to get together." Grant responded:

"Yes This attitude of hers has been passed down to my daughter Tasha. She is consulting a psychoanalyst.

This unbalance state of mind of hers is having a disastrous effect on her son Jonathon. I find them both impossible to deal with. I would leave them both out of my life, but obviously need to leave what fortune I have to her and failing this with her predeceasing Jonathon, all must go to him."

This conversation continued on this level of thinking on both their parts with Mr. Eggleston jotting down notes according to his client's wishes. The morning sun shot beams of light across Mr. Eggleston's desk in front of him. Suddenly the whole matter was becoming very boring to Grant. Alice was dead. She had died a week ago. She had left the whole household without someone to direct the domestic ups and downs at the Great House.

Grant could not do it that was certain. The servants had all loyally attended her funeral service showing due respect. Somehow after Tasha had left home those few years ago when she had married that, who was it . . . . ? Yes. That pilot fellow. The whole involvement had nearly driven he and Alice mad. His son-in-law had flown aircraft in that dreadful German onslaught on to the country's peaceful existence.

He poured the first brandy of the evening after a meal for which he had as usual these days after Alice's demise, little appetite. They had such a routine and quiet existence before the invasion. Then Tasha who had upset the whole family had decided to go into nursing. Alice had been horrified but Tasha with her young set of friends had been adamant that the country's defence system would need some domestic support to the fighting men.

He had now left Mr. Eggleston's rooms and these thoughts had occupied him for the rest of the day until he found himself behind the polished stinkwood desk in the drawing room of the Great House again. He sat there a while mulling over the interview, and then the telephone in the corner suddenly rang. Irritated at having to get up and answer the summons that was being made on him Grant picked up the receiver. Expecting it, and he was right, he heard the impatient though mellow voice of his daughter Tasha.

"Dad. Hullo. How are you? Are you taking mother's death as calmly as possible?"

Grant answered gruffly at her rather forward question typical of his daughter. This was a sensitive family matter.

He spoke into the receiver:

"You know Tasha quite well we were all expecting this to happen. Alice was living a more and more sedentary life. Unhealthy, if you want my honest opinion. She was becoming unrealistic about every single thing that was happening at home here. She was given to hopelessly unbalanced flights of fancy about the great wealth that she and I owned. Now you know Tasha that this is quite untrue."

He paused hearing Tasha speak, then said:

"What is it Tasha?" Was he going deaf? Then he heard her voice. "You know it was because of your increasing lack of communication with her as your lives went on." Tasha he could hear was upset. She continued with the words:

"Dad." To him her voice rasped. "You must put drinking out of your life. This is a bad spell you are going to have to face." He paused then answered:

"Yes I know that Tasha." As usual his soft heartedness flooded over him as he responded to his daughter's words. She would be feeling her mother's loss just as much as he did.

Impatient at his daughter's chiding words he loosened the cord of the telephone and walked over to the settee he had left before it had rung. He settled again comfortably half eased at hearing his daughter's voice. She always had to take the upper hand as a nurse with her parents and now he was at her beck and call.

She was rambling on at the other end of the line as far as he was concerned but then he honed into her words. She was talking about Jonathon her son. What was it she was getting at?

"Father you are not listening as usual I can tell."

There was a pause in their conversation. Idly Grant shook the rose-tinted glass snuffbox turning it upside down. The ring he had been examining yesterday evening fell out and as it did so the diamond came loose from the silver clasps holding it together. Carelessly Grant put all the pieces of the ring into it and closed it.

Almost a shriek came over the line as he tensed. He must not lose the precious stone the large diamond. As he heard again Tasha's voice his mind went back to his engagement with the ring. Then of course his parents had opposed it but Alice the little minx had just twisted them both round her little finger. Tasha's voice came again:

"Are you there, Dad?" "Yes. Yes. I was just handling your late mother's and my engagement ring. The precious stone has just fallen out."

"Dad you must look after it. That is not something men do very well."

Again Grant despised her supercilious attitude. Not usually vindictive he said:

"The ring my dear I have placed in the antique snuff box that your mother gave me as a present on my last birthday while she was alive. It is of special meaning to me."

Then she was taking the upper hand again. She said sharply:

"But mother said I was to have it when she died!" Grant was quick to respond. "Oh no my girl. Together with all the other antiques that your mother collected they will be offered to the local museum." "But why Dad?" "Because my girl I feel it is safest there. I have to see Dr Munro tomorrow and at the last appointment I had with him he was indicating very strongly that I would have to go into a rest home for the aged very soon."

This was true and Grant was trying to avert her sharpness that was her nature as a trained nurse. Surely this would appease her.

There was a pause at the other end of the line that was not surprising after what her father had just said. When this happened as he had intimated to her it would be a big change in the worsening unstable background that she had as a child. Then Tasha said:

"Oh Dad I suppose it won't be that bad." Her parents were always a faint irritation to her so she said a little worried by this news of her father's:

"Right father you organize it. Just be in touch if you need me to wrap up mother's precious antiques. Bill has given me lots of free time and is not demanding of me now. He is also concerned about Jonathon's slightly neurotic behavior. You were also worried about Jonathon's state of mind and senstivity. You seem to be an icon in our son's eyes. Although he is very busy with his studies in Edinburgh right now.

I am finding increased difficulty with my relationships with both Jonathon and his father. Perhaps you could invite him to the Great House for a week this coming vacation and talk some sense into him?" Grant spoke gruffly over the line at this accolade from his daughter in her confidence in him as Jonathon's grandfather:

"Right Tasha I hear your concern about about the lad. I'll contact him for a short visit within the next few days. I have to leave for Dr. Monro in a few minutes this call has held me up already. Goodbye. I will be in touch with you for you assistance in closing down the Great House when the time comes. Goodbye Tasha . . ."

Grant quickly took his walking cane that stood by him near the setee arose and reaching the kitchen in his way out to his appointment, spoke briefly to one of the servants there:

"I am leaving now. I will expect a lunch meal as usual when I return between twelve and on today:

He did not want to upset the newly smooth running of the household that had been reinstated after Alice's passing. He recalled grimly that there had been a short chaotic period of household disorganization after this untimely event.

The two stewards averted their eyes to their immediate tasks they were busy with but stared curiously at the old man as he walked out of the door to leave. They usually knew his movements but he had been unusually brusque this morning and had made no mention of where he was going. Both men felt a vague sense of unease perhaps sensing that their livelihood might be coming to an end.

Grant walked down the driveway from the Great House and opened the little side gate onto the path leading to the village. On arriving at the Doctor's surgery he sat down on a convenient chair and looked interestedly at the two or three folk also waiting to consult the doctor. He was early and tapped his cane impatiently on the wooden floor.

The wait at Doctor Munro's rooms as usual seemed endless. It was hard for him to think at the moment that the doctor had patiently to take his time with the folk consulting him. Again Grant tapped his cane on the floor. His thoughts dwelt on his late wife Alice and then on his grandson Jonathon's problems. Imperceivably though very much in reality there was the sight of Dr. Munro at the open doorway of his surgery.

Grant snapped back into the present situation. Now was his chance. He knew that Doctor Munro was going to chide him about his drinking habits and press him once again over the next few months to make arrangements to empty the Great House of its contents. Also the doctor wanted to persuade him gently but slowly into being admitted into the comfortable rest home on the outskirts of the village where he would not have the pressures and manipulations of social interplay usual for people in his circumstances.

As he entered the consulting room he girded up his mind to put his wants and needs to the good doctor. Before Doctor Munro could push him, even skillfully into anything he did not wish for the doctor greeted him:

"So do we have serious or minor problems today Mr. Godiver?" Grant answered glibly though needing advice and guidance.

"Nothing serious Doctor, no. Of course you know about my wife's death?" "Of course my dear man, of course. This must have left a chaotic situation with her passing. It was quite unexpected her death, yes I do agree." Then after a few moments the doctor took in the physical state of his patient. Yes the doctor thought to himself. Quite clearly a heavy drinker. This habit he would have to halt somehow. He attempted a conversation with Grant:

"You find it lonely now at the Great House being without Alice? That was her name wasn't it?" Grant replied:

Yes. A terrible shock to me. Although she caused me great trouble with her constant wish to collect bric-a-brac. Unfortunately she was living more and more in her imagination as the ageing years crept up on her—and myself with her. She was constantly hinting at these collectibles as being of enormous wealth to us all.

Now as I know you want for me Doctor Munro eventually I will be forced to leave the Great House. Tasha my daughter will have to give up her precious time as a nurse to help me box all these items and either sell them at one of the local venders or put the more valuable of them, that is realistically speaking into the local museum inAlices's memory." He paused looking pained. "It would have broken Alice's heart to know this would happen."

The doctor pursed his lips at this confidence not wanting as was his training to show favoritism to any member of Grant's family, especially as he was fully aware that Grant's daughter was a nurse. So he phrased his one vital question for the consultation:

"My advice is to stop this being out of touch with the reality. I can see your late wife affected your daughter's thinking, also her husband's, with his dangerous pursuits in the wartime. We all have to face reality at some time or other in our lives. With your late wife and you must face it Grant because she is dead now there are no more worries, are there?" Grant responded somewhat queriously to this question by saying:

"I have done a thorough reorganization of the domestic affairs at the Great House but it's not the same without Alice and her continual bringing this or that ornament or picture or other antique home. The Great House is overflowing with them and I have told Tasha my daughter that she or my grandson will have to spend some time with me sorting it all and deciding which items should be personal family hand downs, what should go to the local museum mainly pictures she has unearthed on her outings to the nearby towns or some just to the local junk shop. Otherwise we will just have to throw the rest of the items away. It would have broken Alice's heart."

Doctor Munro somewhat overcome by the situation answered:

"You are getting on now in age. You should take your time about this. The emptying of your mansion of all who live there including you Grant will make Alice's death a reality and force you to realize that you need company. I mean you need the company of those of your own standing. In the long term I mean. Please consider for the future that there does exist a rest home of class for the elderly quite near to the village. No one here knows much about it that is why I am mentioning it to you."

The doctor paused hoping his words would penetrate the rather chaotic time that the old man was living through.

"Yes, yes," said Grant. "But it's my grandson I am concerned about. Alice's handling and manipulation of the whole greater family situation has left Jonathon most sulky and petulant. He is constantly at loggerheads with his mother. As a student he is in a different line of thinking completely. She refuses to accept that he has to study further despite all this apparent great wealth that is completely untrue." Grant looked around suspiciously as if hoping no one could hear. The consultation with the doctor now began to take the form of a friendly chat. Doctor Munro asked Grant:

"Why don't you write to your grandson to stay with you for a while? Then he can help you in your getting rid of the bric-a-brac that you wife has accumulated. Grant answered:

"My daughter has for the last few years steered him away from visiting the Great House because of Alice's influence. I feel this has disrupted the whole family situation. Tasha my daughter is putting on a tough face because of the situation.

I know that Alice has caused Tasha and Jonathon to feel most unbalanced. I can understand this as an older and mature man. On the surface Tasha appears hardened to Jonathon's rudeness but I know her well and I can see that underneath her social play she is one mass of fears and doubts."

Doctor Munro curious in a professional way about this queried:

"Why exactly is this do you think?" Grand replied:

"Well you see Doctor her husband fought on aircraft carriers as a pilot in the last world war. She was in a constant state of anxiety because of this even though she put a brave face on it as a nurse. It took a long time to settle after the wartime though. I don't think that I have even mentioned this to you that she also had the nerve racking experience of being a nurse in the war in London during the German bombing attacks."

Doctor Munro pulled himself up with a start and replied:

"That explains much of your situation to me. I perceive that your grandson must have been brought up as a youngster in a very frightening and uncertain atmosphere. Where is you daughter and her husband now?" Grant answered:

"They live in Ottawa in Canada. I am in constant telephone conversation with Tasha." But I will take your advice and persuade Jonathon to spend some time with me. He is very keen to be in my company as a rule. Although he succeeds in his studies he is inclined to be very unmanageable in social situations. I understand from Tasha that although he is very successful in his studies he is very rude to his fellowmen at the university." The doctor asked:

"What is he studying and where will he be once he has finished? I understand that will be very soon now." Grant said tersely: "He has to be flown out to work on an explorative diamond mining ship off the coast of Sierra Leone in North Africa."

The conversation between the two men lapsed into silence. Grant had for the last few minutes been seeking a way to finish the interview. Now was his chance. He rose from the chair suddenly saying and taking the upper hand in the relationship.

"I'll be off, now doctor. I have noted what you have said regarding my family and my future and I will give it considerable thought. It will take time as you say."

Grant turned and unobtrusively left the surgery. A few curious glances from the locals awaiting their turn with Doctor Munro followed him. He decided on the walk back to the Great House in the warmth of the later morning with birds singing all around him in the country air that he would give Jonathon a call. Oh! Where was it that he had put the telephone number of his grandson's university residence!

Yes, in the lower drawer of his antique desk the one Alice had persuaded him to buy a few years ago. He was greeted humbly by the two menservants at the front door but made his way straight to the old fashioned desk. Carefully, because it was a desk that was past its prime he opened the drawer where he remembered putting Jonathon's telephone number. He ruffled through some of the other documents lying in the sweet-smelling musty old compartment and came across the piece of paper he was looking for.

Ah! He took it out and walked over to the telephone. It was going on lunchtime so Jonathon ought to be through with his morning lectures. The number was quite clear on the slightly crumpled paper. He dialed. Some young idiot without a clue about Grant's asking to speak to his grandson answered. He had to ask and explain several times before it was clear to the young student who had answered, that he wanted Jonathon Albany to be called to the telephone.

Then there was silence on the other end of the telephone connection to Edinburgh. Suddenly a crackling sound of a voice that slowly became recognizable to Grant as that of his grandson came over the line. Vague as the young are, Grant thought to himself when the obvious question came through the telephone to him:

"Who is there?" Grant said urgently: "Jonathon? Is that Jonathon?" The voice that sounded on the other end of the line came through most hesitantly: "Hullo! Hullo! Granddad? Is that you?" Grant spoke to the point.

"Of course it is son. You should recognize my voice by now. I have a request to offer you. You know your late grandmother, my wife Alice was an incorrigible collector of bric-a-brac that is of little value? That was items and also articles and curiosities of some little more worth that were eye-catching? These were in fact cheap goods that took her fancy. Now Jonathon . . . ." His grandson's voice broke in but before he could make his grandfather aware that he had something to say Grant continued, anxious now to make the most of the fact that he had indeed actually managed to track down his grandson in the midst of a student's day

"Jonathon, I want you to come and spend a week or two here with me at the Great House. I know your vacation is coming up soon. Surely you can spare me the time?" He paused wondering if his plea to his grandson was going to have any effect on Tasha's, his daughter's, son. The muffled low voice of the young man came down over the air:

"Yes grandfather. I know your servants always produce very tasty meals. For that alone I will make sure I will be able to be with you." Grant responded immediately at the success of his invitation. The young he had found were highly unpredictable but he had timed his call aright.

"Great, son." Then Jonathon's voice came over the line again. "But why do you want me at the Great House granddad? There is nothing I can think of that I can do to keep me busy." Grant again answered quickly:

"But there is son. I would like you to help me box all Alice's collectibles. It seems from what my doctor has told me that sometime in the next six months I will have to be admitted to a rest home where there is nursing care for the elderly. You see son I cannot leave here with the Great House full to overflowing with all you late grandmother's acquisitions." He paused again and hearing no response from the other end of the line said:

Hullo Jonathon? Are you still there?"

He knew his grandson would not be too keen on any form of physical activity such as his grandfather was asking of him so an idea came to mind. He suggested:

"Jonathon? You can choose and have to keep or to sell any of the collectibles that I have here at the moment if you help. Then a hesitant and not fully enthusiastic voice came back to him:

"Alright Granddad I'll be there in just over a weeks time. I have finished my studies finally now and will just have to pack and say my farewells at the study centre here."

Grant awoke later in the morning. He enquired manservant who waited on him at breakfast:

"So he's gone has he?" "Yes sir." The man said. "He left in the Great House's automobile at first light. As you know sir, it's an hour of two's journey to the central city of London." Grant responded "How was he looking and behaving my man? I am very anxious about him. He is in a highly unbalanced state of mind. He should not be going on this jaunt, this wild goose chase. It is a highly dangerous scheme but the youngster seems to be totally unaware of this."

The man he was addressing said: "But it is his job his future occupation. He will be paid well for what he does. And he has high qualifications too from what he says. He is a clever lad."

Grant was mollified. It was his appointment with the lawyer this morning. He tried to remember what he had decided about the will last evening. Dash it the brandies had completely clouded his memory about his decision. Perhaps he should cancel Mr Framby and call in tomorrow he would have the minimum to drink tonight, this evening and then spend the early night hours while waiting in the time before retiring to bed, deciding definitely what he would do about the inheritance that he would leave after his death.

These thoughts occupied him until in his thinking over the matter were completely disturbed by the ugly jangling of his telephone. It was of course his daughter. She would of course thanks to Alice's dreamy state of unreal living, be in a complete state of nerves about her son Jonathon's departure. That did mean though that she felt very strongly about her son. But Tasha was a nurse. She had chosen that calling. Why did she personally have such an emotional time dealing with Jonathon's interests.

"Dad is that you?" Tasha's nerve wracked voice came over the line. "I am in a complete state of upheaval because of this dangerous mission that Jonathon is undertaking. Has he gone? He is not in a stable state of reason to do this. I am both a nurse and his mother and I completely disapprove if it. Isn't it bad enough to have lived with his father targeting then U-boats from the aircraft carriers in the World War. I lived through all that and now Jonathon has to do this to me!"

CHAPTER 2

The rest of the spring day passed slowly. Idly during the afternoon after his customary rest after an appetizing lunch Grant stumbled around the rooms picking up item after item that Alice had bought in her visits to the surrounding villages. What was the point of it all? She was dead now.

He was so overcome by her passing since it happened those two months ago that he realized that he had not even been aware of how the bric-a-brac had been accumulating in the Great House. He recalled how her voice had constantly been chiding the two men-servants responsible for their domestic care. Her voice seemed real in his memory:

"Grant, that china figurine does not look its best placed right next to the ornate antique clock I bought two weeks ago. Have you got no sense of the attractive placing of my ornaments? The three brass monkeys with their labels Hear No Evil, See No Evil, Speak No Evil. These look quite wrong placed right at the edge of the mantelpiece.

Didn't you know I would have wanted these as a centerpiece? But you would not have understood the humorous message they give out to you and I or any of our visitors. The grandfather clock? Has it been moved again? And why does the cuckoo clock have to be right next to it? And my china mugs and toby jug?"

Grant felt his self-control going as the remembrance of her slightly grating voice, nerve-wracking to him in his old age came back to his mind. Could he even admit to himself, yes it is a relief that she has gone. Angrily he thought assertively yes, I am glad our marriage is all over. And while she was alive between them it was always agreed that it was he who was going to be the first to go in their togetherness.

Evening was drawing on. He felt the old familiar longing for supper and his usual brandies to make the evening less lonely. Giles appeared through the doorway and obsequiously as usual asked:

"Are you ready for your preprandial sherry with the savory biscuits that you enjoy so?"

Grand mumbled ungrateful sounding thanks for the thoughtfulness that the valet had shown. He nibbled a few of the appetizers then stretched his hand out for his cane stick to help him to the dining room. Bad-temperedly he thought to himself, yes I am feeling my age.

He tried once or twice to raise himself from the setee. The valet on seeing that the old man was trying hard to be independent in his present actions said encouragingly:

"You will manage it. There you are, nearly up."

Grant could not manage after three or four attempts at getting up. The supper that he knew was waiting for him gave him extra strength but the valet knew that he would have to help his master. He chided gently:

"Come now Mr. Godiver. Do not shrug off help from me any longer. See, I'll help you."

Grant said sulkily:

"Yes my man. You knew that I could walk didn't you? It's my back and legs though. Weak all of a sudden."

The valet smiled in the patience that he was showing towards the old man:

"On your way now sir. Supper is waiting."

There were not many such days now before Jonathon's arrival. One morning after a while there was a tremendous commotion in the front driveway and then at the front door and finally in the hallway. A voice that he recognized as his grandson's, Jonathon's was heard, sounding disorderly and loud in ordering Giles as to the bringing in of three or four of valises and a set of golf clubs. Dash it thought Grant as he manoevered himself from the breakfast table to use what was left in his bodily strength to control the situation and welcome his grandson to the Great House.

He had limped to the hallway and the chaotic scene met his eyes. The golf bag was lying on its side one or two clubs having fallen out of the container. One of the valises had fallen open and some crumpled and dirty clothes were tumbling out onto the floor. Without even welcoming his grandson, Grant after addressing this sight said angrily:

"No, no Jonathon. This will not do at all."

Jonathon only slowly beginning to be aware of the querulous old man who was his grandfather, was entering in by the doorway. He stared again at the disorganized sight on the floor. Jonathon said to Giles:

"No man I said that other valise must be brought in first. Not that one. I told you that the lock on that one was loose. Now see what has happened."

He indicated the rather messy sight on the floor of the hallway to the Great House. Fully having lost his temper Jonathon added:

"And I cannot wait while you clear this all up. Are you bringing in the other two cases soon?" The poor servant who would need time to clear all the untidy disorder and take all Jonathon's possessions to the room prepared or him upstairs, said patiently:

"Just you go ahead to meet your grandfather. Ah! There he is, waiting for you."

Jonathon then focused his attention on the old man who was his grandfather. He thought to himself. He looks so old. Even older than I have ever seen him before. The aged man addressed his grandson:

"Greetings my lad. I am glad to see you. You seem to be having no little trouble with your luggage." Grant balanced himself on his cane stick as he caught the bad tempered sound of Jonathon's surly words:

"Hullo Granddad." Then he said sarcastically: "This is the best these servants could do to bring in my possessions from the car outside?"

Grant's valet looked shiftily at the old man. Was he in trouble again? Grant responded covering the situation:

"Anyway it's all inside now. My valet will take it all upstairs to the bedroom the servants have prepared for you. Come into the lounge my lad."

Jonathon looked doubtful at leaving his golf clubs and valises but subserviently followed his grandfather into the living quarters. His first remark was:

"There seem to be more ornaments and objèts d'art than ever here. My grandmother must have been on several more spending sprees since I was here last year. But I understand that she has died now. I had the news at my university hostel some months ago shortly after it happened. You must be very lonely now."

Jonathon was feeling a trifle guilty at his attitude on first arriving. Grant replied tersely:

"Yes that is so. But the reason that I summoned you here is to help me pack away all these useless items of you grandmother's and distribute them to curiosity shops and the rarer items to the local museum."

Jonathon groaned at this news. Grant ignored this reaction and just continued:

"Yes. You can unpack and report to me here after breakfast tomorrow to begin boxing up the items. They will all have to be wrapped carefully. It will all be finished within a week with your help. I cannot trust the servants to do this and anyway they are too busy."

He continued talking now on a different track:

"Your mother. How is her health?" Jonathon grimaced and said:

You can well ask that Granddad. She is as difficult as ever. Nothing I can do is good enough for her. In the diplomatic corps with my father they have recently visited South Africa. A family with a daughter she thinks has great personality and attractiveness has taken her fancy. You know that I am to go into the employment of a diamond mining company both on a ship off the coast of Sierra Leone in North Africa, testing geologically for these precious mineral gems, and later off the coast of Namibia as well.

I will have periods of off duty as paid for leave in lodging quarters in Cape Town. My mother is gushing over the fact that I must meet and get to know Marijke, these new acquaintances' daughter. Her father is a wealthy gold mining magnate."

Yes that's all very well Jonathon. I am sure that you are quite excited about your future and looking forward to it also."

Grant spoke to his grandson after leading him into what was now his privacy of the drawing room out of the earshot of the servants. There were no females in the Great House now. Alice was dead and Tasha had left home many years ago. He tried to put Jonathon at his ease but could see a selfish frown in his grandson's forehead and a sulky look playing around his lips. It all added up to a very spoilt upbringing. Why had Tasha raised her son so?

Hints of what his wife Alice had been played around Grant's thoughts. Grant was sure that he knew what was best for the young man. Perhaps he could find out why the youth was behaving like this. So he spoke to Jonathon with a plan in mind:

"As usual at this time after supper I sit down trying to relax for the evening with a brandy or two."

The old man walked over to a glass fronted cabinet at the side of the lounge bent down and took out two brandy glasses and a bottle of the finest and most expensive brandy available. He was going to use an offer of a companionable drink to elicit from his grandson what his flare-ups were all about:

"Be seated Jonathon. I am sure you won't refuse this after-dinner sustenance that I am offering you?" Jonathan took a look at the shining glasses. Grant began to pour a small amount into each glass. Gruffly Jonathan said:

"That will help Granddad. I have just come out of an excruciatingly difficult year at the University in Scotland. Not only were the examination papers set for the class deliberately tricky but I have been pestered all year by the girls who attended the study center with me although they were all much younger. They will never learn. It was a difficult year socially as a result but I think that I have made the grade. I am only too pleased to be finished with it."

Grant said to him trying to knock some sense into the lad. As his grandfather he could only see matters with his own great age preventing him from understanding what it was that was bugging the youngster:

"What is making you so angry Jonathon?" The young man answered:

"It is my mother Granddad. She is constantly telephoning me wanting to know every detail about what I do. As if it wasn't enough that I was keen on one particular girl at the university with others of them taking my mind off my studies. Tasha has, as I have told you already acquainted herself with a wealthy family in South Africa where I will be working eventually. I do not want my girlfriend Jean to know about this daughter of theirs Marijke of whom Tasha thoroughly approves. This is not what I want. My mother is becoming impossible."

Grant swiveled the brandy around at the bottom of the polished glass in his right hand. Jonathon somewhat new to the art of drinking half-heartedly did the same looking into the contents of the pear shaped glass as he did so. He was as yet uncertain of a start of an imbibing habit for himself. He knew several of the more rowdy students at the university involved themselves in this but though it irritated him somehow he felt safe in his old grandfather's company. Grant said to him:

"I can see you are bothered and uncertain about our family situation. What I want to know is why are you feeling this way?"

Jonathon put on a stubborn look to his face. His family had been good to him seeing him successfully through his studies. There was though a feeling of instability filtering through from his grandmother Alice's generation right through to his own. Why was this? He just could not put his thoughts into words. Grant though had spent much time with Alice, and Jonathon as a youngster and could see immediately what the problem was. He said candidly:

"I know Jonathon. It is your grandmother who is the cause of all this in her increasing attitude of unreality to life. Your mother Tasha was a flighty young woman I'll say it myself even though she is my daughter. She was a blonde and as a result had just far too many suitors. They just never seemed to leave her alone and of course in the household set it meant that Alice your grandmother and I were constantly being disturbed by her friends.

Then being popular at school she was earmarked for going into nursing where she succeeded wholly. Then the war came and she fell in love with that pilot fellow Andrew who was your father. He as you know had a distinguished flying career on the aircraft carriers in the north sea hunting the German U-boats."

Here Jonathon broke in eagerly at the mention of his father:

"Yes, my father was someone of intensely high standards. So was my mother. I found it constantly difficult as a growing person to keep up with their fast flow of verbal interplay and as is usual I suppose in a family the inevitable bickering that went with it. I tried to keep my mind going as fast as their conversation and that of their friends but eventually I gave up and took to sulking and rudeness because of their lack of patience. I find it difficult to relate to my friends so-called as a result and am becoming more and more introverted." His grandfather answered:

"Jonathon, Jonathon life is always difficult. Speaking as someone who has been through it all and now am reaching my end I give you the heartfelt advice not to take yourself too seriously. Sometimes I think of my life as being like going somehow from the tip of one iceberg to the next. You will sink into icecold water if you don't. Life is made for us in that way I feel sometimes."

Jonathon slowly came out of his pensive almost sulky state and spoke after a few moments:

"That's difficult Granddad. For me at any rate. My studies were not only boring but because they were I was becoming withdrawn. I did have a purpose but now know that I must snap out of it all with an exciting marine exploration coming up when I'm through helping you with my Grandmother's collectibles. It's sad that she is no more isn't it?"

Grant sniffed his brandy to try and pretend he wasn't missing his late wife and said slowly:

"Yes and no to that Jonathon. Alice was quite troublesome towards the end of her life. Her unrealistic attitude was being passed down the generations and was beginning to hit us all in one way or another. But don't let you and I become morbid. There is a lot of life left for you especially. Where is the mining company taking you? You leave by air in two weeks to fulfill your bursary obligations I think you told me when I spoke to you on the telephone. Are you nervous?"

"No Granddad. It's just that it will be an all male scenario. The young girls did at least give some lightheartedness to the study situation but they were very distracting," said Jonathon. Grant responded quickly. "Hasn't Tasha any ideas for a permanent relationship of the opposite sex for you? Both you and I know that your parents lead a very social life after being in the diplomatic corps all these years."

Jonathon looked confused Grant could see. Briefly he tried to put his mind back in his life to the time he was Jonathon's age. Yes it had been chaotic as a young man as regards the opposite sex. He meditated briefly that life doesn't change over the generations. Here was this young man experiencing just what he had felt those many years ago. But then there had come into his life his wife Alice. It seemed as if this whole experiences flashed through his brain.

No he must not think like that. That was the way Tasha had told him that the doctors and nurses said happened when you were dying. No, he definitely was not on his deathbed yet. Jonathon spoke breaking the silence. His face Grant could see clearly told of being desperate to confide in someone. So Grant looked enquiringly at him waiting for the words to come out:

"You see Granddad it is all to do with my girlfriend. She is a young Scottish lass but there have been many students where I have been studying who have distracted me vying for my attention. They do not know about our friendship, mine and Jean's, but I have managed to keep my mind on my studies luckily and have finished studying now and am ready to face the world outside, with the work that I have to undertake."

Grant looked appeased at this news and asked:

"What is the work you are going to pursue, Jonathon? You did tell me that but in my old age it has slipped my mind what with your Grandmother's passing." "Yes I did tell you," said Jonathon. "I am being flown out to Sierra Leone to be transported onto a ship that is doing deep sea mining research underwater off the coast of the north west African state. I have a contract to fulfil now that I have a bursary to repay that I had for my studies. It is my intention to go about this whole undertaking very thoroughly and it will be quite a dangerous expedition."

Grant looked apprehensive at hearing the bare facts of what Jonathon was going to be doing and responded to this by saying:

"To take your mind off this briefly . . . has your mother got any plans for a female partner for you?"

Grant was purposely trying to take his grandson's mind off the present amorous situation in Jonathon's life, because it did not look as if there was any future in his current relationship for the present. He reflected that young people had very fleeting cross gender associations of which he could see was the case with his grandson.

Jonathon looked relieved to have someone older, actually his Grandfather of whom he was very fond anyway, taking an interest in this aspect of his life. He was a good looking young man Grant thought to himself reflecting briefly on his own life at his grandson's young age. Seeing the attentive response he was getting from the old man he confided:

"These young girls at the university I found quite a nuisance Granddad."

Then he clammed up again. Did this older person really understand his position? Grant also as a man, though older by far was short for words. His mind was slowing up as he should have told the doctor yesterday but he felt a surge of envy towards the young man. He would have loved to have all that attention from young women when he was a youth. But it had not been possible. His own father had died at an early age and he had been forced to take on the management domestically and financially of the Great House. His thoughts jumped back to the present. Then he spoke:

"Jonathon you are lucky to have had so many friends of whatever sex. As a man of great age as far as you are concerned, although matters and circumstances are different in this generation of the family that you find yourself in you ought to take full advantage of your social life." Jonathon broke into these words finding them just as heavy going as the place of study that he had quitted within the last few weeks.

"Granddad, it is Jean who is important to me now. But it seems that I will be away from her almost permanently now because after the training spell with the diamond mining company aboard ship off the West African state of Sierra Leone then I am due to go on with the training on a diamond mining barge off the Orange River mouth in the southern West of South Africa. This is a permanent post. I will get leave, yes but Granddad it seems that my mother wants to involve me in a wealthy gold mining family's life there.

My mother is quite entranced with their daughter Marijke and is keen for me to meet her on shore leave in Cape Town." Grant said:

"I had no idea Tasha has been in South Africa. So this is what she has been up to. Always difficult, Tasha your mother. She is too adventurous by far, being egged on by your father with his air force background over the North Atlantic icy wastes during the last war. The whole situation in the family especially with Alice's continual slide into a less and less state of instability and unreality before her death is causing the whole family to get more and more out of control.

You see Jonathon there was a need for Alice to keep her mind off the ageing process that everyone goes through eventually in life. She was a sensitive person and found it hard to control Tasha your mother. Your mother Tasha, when the second world war descended on us here in England because of the pressure put on her by her schoolfriends, was encouraged, I would say almost forced to go into nursing.

Tasha like Alice was easily upset as a young girl, but I will say it Jonathon, she had a tough streak in her nature that her mother Alice found hard to bear as one who doted on her daughter. When she had her nursing diploma the German bombing began and she had no choice but for to obey orders and put all she had into her nursing care expertise in the blitz in London. I too found it hard to bear knowing Tasha's life was at stake at any moment during those war years.

Alice of course was nearly frantic every day we lived through at that time and it was all I could do to control her. I think it was at this time that her mind gave in. Of course Tasha, on the infrequent visits that she was able to make down to the Great House here found no support in what she was doing from her mother. Being in one another's company only seemed to worsen their situation. I as Tasha's father could see my daughter's nerves were at breaking point especially towards the end of the fighting when she met her husband your father the flyer." Here Jonathon broke in:

"Yes, my parents did not talk much about those years but the tension was there because of the constant dangers and risks my father experienced targeting the U-boats over the icy waters of the north Atlantic sea. All he experienced did not help my mother's nervous state and I was left to my own devices as a growing lad and became lonely and introverted. I had few friends in my school years and only branched out later socially a little as a student."

All this while they were talking Jonathon was wrapping ornament after ornament of his late grandmother's collection. She had built it up so lovingly, the young man knew. Grant had asked one of the men servants to provide the tough wrapping paper. During the mornings of Jonathon's stay there were soon six or seven boxes full of these all neatly tied up ready for the auctioneers and the local museum. Of course no one knew but it was nearly breaking Grant's heart.

Gradually the silence of boredom fell on the countryside around the Great House and upon Grandfather and Grandson sitting in the lounge. One of the menservants knocked unobtrusively and entered. The weather was chill. He said:

"At your pleasure sir, I'll light the log fire."

Disturbed momentarily in the peace that had fallen over the centuries old Great House the birds outside having stopped in their twittering, evening drew on. Dishes and pots and pans could be heard faintly the sounds coming from the kitchen. Jonathon Grant thought glancing at the young man off and on now seemed downhearted, confused and anxious. Grant finding voice to speak to his Grandson spoke, breaking the pall of silence. The supper must be cooking. Whiffs of roast meat drifted into the room.

"How can I be of help to you Jonathon? You know what the family means to me. We have always been a close-knit knot. I am aware that Alice's worsening mental state made us all uncertain of ourselves. For all her unbalanced frame of mind she seemed to control us all.

Your mother Tasha tried to put her in her place but Alice was too clever for that. She and Tasha just began to live separate lives when your mother married. Tasha's experiences in the wartime just made Alice's neurotic state even worse. When she and your father arrived on their less and less frequent visits to the Great House, I was the one who had to keep my head and control their constant infighting." Jonathon in his depression answered his Grandfather:

"When I was at school I was constantly aware of the unstable influence they were having on my life. I turned to my books of learning especially those to do with science. I was constantly teased, unmercifully so, and could not find true friends amongst my schoolmates.

The only thing that did not suffer was my studies. I was given a study award but felt maladjusted right through my post school studies and now have to face the reality of a few months of being aboard a ship off the West African country of Sierra Leone. I did tell you about this Granddad. Grant and Jonathon had now finished supper and were sharing the usual brandies in front of the log fire.

Jonathon also was gradually seeing crumble all that he had known on vacations as a youngster in his Grandparents' Great House as he worked the following day slowly and patiently in the boxing process of Alice's remaining collectibles. This only served to worsen his depression. He was down at heart at the thought of having to forget about Jean his girlfriend and suddenly silence fell on the two of them as lunch time approached. Grant with a perseverance he had always tried to muster in his life could sense his grandson's mood. Jonathon confided:

"I am so uncertain of the future, Granddad. The company who gave me the study award are requiring me to work at testing the sea bed off the north west African coast of Sierra Leone. For all I have studied in geology I feel helpless in this undertaking. Oh! I realize there will be others to help in the beginning but I have the constant nagging in my mind of my father's experiences on the aircraft carriers over the North Atlantic Ocean as one of the pilots.

My mother tried after the war to be a constant support to him but intense anxiety was caused her at work in the Blitz as a nurse in London while my father was on active service. This caused me an only child to have a very highly-strung nature. The diplomatic corps that were part of their life afterwards left them little time for me. My growing years were very lonely."

Grant responded to this confidence:

"Yes son I did have some sort of idea as to the pain caused to you as a teenager especially. Tasha your mother was always difficult as a young girl although she was very reliable. She could put her mother in her place."

Grant suppressed a grim chuckle. It had always given him secret pleasure after their marriage had progressed all those many years ago to see how Alice his wife had sulked at Tasha's continual taking of the upper hand with her mother while she was growing up. He again spoke out his thoughts:

"But Tasha also had her sensitive side that was gradually hurt more and more as she tried to cope in the war situation. Quite honestly as I know her now she is just a bundle of nerves."

He did not want to say to Jonathon at present that her son's employment in West Africa was just making it worse for her. This conversation about the greater family continued into lunch and the afternoon and a couple more of the boxes were tied up with the tough string.

Jonathon was looking more and more confused in fact quite crestfallen. His Grandfather sensed his mood. In a habit of positive thinking, jocular style a discipline in his nature that he had personally and carefully cultivated especially in heart affairs of the family he spoke in a fruity tone:

"I know it's all very serious when you are a young man." These encouraging words did nothing to lift the depressed and dull senses that being out of his student atmosphere had left him with. He had hardly heard his Grandfather's voice let alone taken in anything the now aging man had said.

His thoughts were mostly centered on Jean his girlfriend. Grant tried to break into the youngster's consciousness by saying: "Come now Jonathon. It can't be that bad. After your spell here helping to shut up the old house you and I know so well and . . . ." he paused a spate of thoughtfulness seeping into his brain. "And the people we remember who have passed through it."

Here he walked over to the drinks cabinet and gingerly took out the brandy decanter and two brandy glasses. He said again:

"Come Grandson! We'll have a snifter or two and look to see what the future holds for both of us."

Jonathon did not look any the more pleased at this action of his Grandfather's mainly because it had become a principle of his not to indulge, or rather over indulge in such imbibing. He had never been part of the normal roistering of the students and their social behavior at the university.

As his Grandfather handed him a glass with a little liquid in it for him to savor his thoughts surfaced to the present. He knew he must pull himself together. He must tell this old Grandfather of his that he had a 'plane to catch within the week that would take him down to Freetown in Sierra Leone on the West African coast to the north of the continent. Slowly he spoke as the fumes of the liquor met his taste buds and nostrils.

"Yes Granddad. I know all about the family problems only too well. My mother and father have nearly destroyed my life. To add to all this I will probably never see Jean again." Grant was immediately interested. "And who is Jean?" He joked.

Grant could see that his grandson was more than a little upset. He questioned him as the days went on before he left for West Africa on what should have been a stirring adventure for a youngster The old man knew however that it would mean careful and hard work for all on the ship that Jonathon would be aboard, investigating the seabed off Sierra Leone hoping to find a diamond bearing area there to mine. The conversation fell onto how the youngster was feeling about the venture. Grant said:

"You will be taken to Freetown by 'plane. How do you feel about this? I know that you have never flown before." Jonathon replied:

"It's not that Granddad. It's my mother's attitude to the whole contract situation. She is panicking not realizing the security that the company affords. She thinks that it will be far too dangerous." Grant asked: "I do understand her feelings but what is the alternative for you? You have to have some sort of income don't you?" Jonathon replied glumly indicating to Grant that he would like to follow his mother's wishes for him to take a land based job in a firm dealing with mining geology that was his qualification, in South Africa a mineral rich country.

"Behind the whole problem of where I am employed is my situation regarding Jean my girlfriend. I know my university days are over now but I would like to stay in touch with her. This will be impossible because my work is going to take me out of Great Britain To add to the situation Tasha has a young woman acquaintance lined up for me in South Africa."

Grant stifle a smile at the earnestness of the young man's amours but went on to say:

"Yes, Jonathon I am very aware that Tasha's, your mother's neuroses have been inherited by your late grandmother. Alice was quite neurotic and unbalanced towards the end of her life. It was sad to see the way she died. She had been quite overcome with Tasha's activities in the blitz as a nurse in London in the wartime.

Neither I nor your grandmother knew if we were ever going to see our daughter your mother again from minute to minute as the hours ticked by here at the Great House in the country with the distant whining in the distance of the enemy 'planes overheard. Tasha was involved in the care of those hurt in the air raids over the city.

It seems to me that you have inherited these unstable feelings. Tasha was never the same after the war although it always appeared that she put on a tough face to everyone she come into contact with socially afterwards when it was all over. But back to the present. You say that your flight leaves from a private aerodrome the day after tomorrow?"

Chapter 3

Jonathon went to bed that night feeling a little comforted by his confiding in his grandfather as he had done from a very young age. Nothing seemed right though without his beloved grandmother Alice. And it seemed also that he was going to have to be in Africa for good now from very soon. How was he going to keep in touch with Jean now?

These were the finishing thoughts of the day, very depressing. He awoke even more downcast. He had been notified that the especially charted flight for Freetown the capitol of Sierra Leone was leaving at 2 p.m. The train to London left at 8 in the morning. He lifted one eye open to a steady drizzle outside the window that must have been slightly opened earlier on by one of the menservants as there was a cold draft.

He cast a glance over to the light valise that he would be taking on the 'plane with him. He had been warned not to bring too much gear. Quickly his thoughts were being activated in his mind, that had been carefully trained for the employment he was undertaking on board ship of the West African coast.

The few documents necessary for his registration with the company stood there alongside the valise. Awakening more rapidly now he felt hunger pangs hit him. He and Grant had few words though to pass one to the other over the breakfast table. Grant finished eating and informed his grandson:

"I have ordered the car to take you to the airport. Or if you like you can take the train."

Grateful for the use of the automobile Jonathon plumped for his grandfather's convenient offer. He said:

"Well now granddad I'll be off. I am not going to be sentimental about leaving. This departure is for good. I will be spending some time with Jean before I board the flight."

Although these words were jaunty enough Grant could see that his grandson was confused and crestfallen at having to leave the Great House seemingly as life was taking him. Jonathon climbed into the little vehicle and was on his way.

He had arranged to meet Jean at a certain tearoom to have some time together before finally parting. He told the chauffeur to drop him in the vicinity of their meeting place. Then he walked trying not drag his feet in the desperation and uncertainty that he was experiencing at leaving Jean in England until a time in the future that he was as yet aware of.

He was feeling with all the despondency and uncertainty also quite confused by the present changing circumstances. For all that he was enduring with his mother's attitude he still felt a robust manhood within his being. He knew Jean would be waiting in the little Lyons teahouse, she had promised and he knew even in his own maturity that she would not let him down.

He had told her a time to meet and where but she had said she would not be able to make it to the private airport to see him off. These thoughts were with him on this fair to middling warm to sunny day that he was leaving England in. Anxiety nagged at him though. He arrived outside the little tearoom. Would she be there, looking as chic as usual with that covert though inviting smile playing around her lips? In the intimacy of their friendship he wondered which of them would spot the other first.

Then he heard her voice high but mellifluous and familiar too, coming from one corner of the tearoom. She was dressed warmly but simply and her slightly curling light brown hair was neatly drawn back from her face in a black velvet ribbon. Her words came tumbling out:

"Jon! How good it is to see you." As he had perceived as a student mixing with both genders of young people, females always talked the most even to the point of having the last word, not to mention the last laugh in conversations with the opposite sex. So he went on after her rather uncertain though carefully thought out greeting:

"Hullo Jean! So it's the last we will be together for a long time isn't it?" She replied after he had seated himself opposite her:

"Don't even stress that point Jon. I don't know now what I am going to do in my spare time without you. I have found a job as an au pair in provincial France. I will be putting my mind to that and hope that I will hear from you by letter from time to time." Jonathon replied:

"Yes, Jean, I do promise to be in touch. He stifled a grin. She was taking this so seriously. "Our friendship is too valuable to be put at stake. I will miss Great Britain and you. Although I am feeling quite unable to predict the future, I know that I must persevere with my geological work at sea. I do feel the situation, the exploration of the mining of the seabed as quite dicey, even dangerous. My mother is going through a very anxious time because of what I am undertaking. Also it is all happening in one of those politically unstable West African states, Sierra Leone."

Grant awoke later in the morning He enquired of his manservant who waited on him at breakfast:

"So he's gone has he?" "Yes sir. He left in the Great House's automobile at first light. As you know sir it's an hour or two's journey to the central city of London." Grant queried of the man: "How was he looking and behaving? I am very anxious about him." The servant answered: "He seemed very worried too sir. In my humble opinion sir he should not be going on this jaunt, this scheme but the youngster seems to be totally unaware of it." The manservant he was addressing continued:

"But it is his job his future occupation. He will be paid well for what he does. And he has high qualifications too from what he says. He is a clever lad."

Grant was mollified. It was his appointment with the lawyer this morning. He tried to remember what he had decided about his will last evening. Dash it, the brandies had completely clouded his memory about his decision. Perhaps he should contact Mr. Egglestone and call in the day after. He would have the minimum to drink tonight this evening and then spend the early night hours while waiting in the lonely time before retiring to bed, deciding definitely exactly what he would do about the inheritance that he would leave after his death.

These thoughts occupied him until his thinking over the matter was completely disturbed by the ugly jangling of his telephone. It was of course his daughter. She would naturally thanks to Alice's dreamy state of unreality, be in a complete state of nerves about her son Jonathon's departure. That did mean though that she felt very strongly about him.

However Tasha was a nurse. She had chosen that calling. Why did she personally have such an emotional time dealing with Jonathon's interests? Her voice cut into his already anxious state:

"Dad is that you?" Tasha's nerve racked voice came over the telephone line. "I am in a complete state of upheaval because of this dangerous mission that Jonathon is undertaking. Has he gone yet? He is not in a stable state of reason to do this. I am both a nurse and his mother and I completely disapprove of it. Isn't it bad enough to have to have lived with his father targeting the U-boats from the aircraft carriers in the war? I lived through all that you know, and now Jonathon has to do this to me."

Grant drew in his breath. This was yet another of Tasha's complaining calls to him. At least her mother the dear departed Alice had kept a wave of cheerfulness going for all her increasing flight into unreality towards the end of her life. He then spoke at a moment after what seemed to him like a string of words from her without any meaning:

"Tasha my dear Jonathon has already left. He went up to London just this morning. I will agree with you he does seem very despondent and unwilling to go because of your feeling about this but I think that has to do with his current girlfriend Jean. She is a Scottish lass that he met while studying. Has he told you about her?"

A cough sounded over the line. So Tasha was smoking again. Knowing his daughter he could judge that she was at the end of her tether at what her son was doing. Then he again heard her voice:

"But Dad didn't I tell you about this marvelous couple and their daughter that I met when I was with Owen this year on a diplomatic visit to South Africa? You do recall that Owen is my husband don't you?" Grant snapped at her for all his dotage: "I am not senile yet Tasha!" At this there was the expected silence at the other end as he had predicted to himself. She continued after a pause:

"My personal reason for going on the visit and I didn't have to, Owen could have handled it alone, was to prepare the way for Jonathon. You do know that after his time in Sierra Leone he is to be based on a diamond mining barge off the coast of South West Africa?" Dad, couldn't you have stopped all this? The political situation in that country is totally unstable with child soldiers and an uncertain and unreliable government there. The whole place is totally third world."

Grant again sucked in his breath. Yes he was out of touch with what in reality was transpiring in his grandson's life but there was nothing that he could have done to stop what was happening. So he reverted to the subject of Jean Jonathon's girlfriend. This was totally against Tasha's wishes. He spoke tersely:

"You know Tasha, to interfere in the love lives of young men is very dangerous emotionally for them. Jean is the one stable part of his life. He is going into an unknown situation and is quite nervous about it as well as you have picked up in his situation. Just leave that part of Jonathon's life alone Tasha. He is at this moment having a farewell celebration with Jean in London."

Then there was silence between the old man and his daughter on the line both being emotionally upset by Tasha's flare-up about her son. Grant heard the receiver on the other end of the line click down. Tasha he knew would be in tears. He felt helpless. What could he have done to stop Jonathon from taking up this job. His subconscious came to the fore in his mind. Yes it would be a very dangerous mission.

But Jonathon was young and Grant knew the capacity the young had for excitement and adventure. From what he had read in the newspapers it seemed there was almost constant civil war going on in that part of Africa the north west where the continent jutted out in a continental bulge. He felt helpless for a minute also, then thought to himself: but the youngster will be working aboard a large ship off the coast dredging the sea floor for diamond bearing matter.

Jonathon had done courses in geology and marine mathematics so would be working away from the trouble if any, at the time of his stay in Sierra Leone. No, he would telephone Tasha in a day or two and put the reality of the situation to her. It was not a good feeling for him to know Tasha, his daughter was suffering like this.

At the time of his conversation with his daughter Jonathon had met up with Jean his student day girlfriend in the Lyons corner teahouse where they would be together for a farewell. They had both been studying at the same university for the last three years and were also very close friends. He saw Jean immediately upon entering the tearoom and glanced around the near empty but cosy place:

"Jean," he spoke crisply knowing that she would be thrilled to see him after only two weeks. They had both graduated on the same day. Jean spoke a little timidly: "Did it go well then your helping your grandfather with the final boxing? How is he taking your grandmother's death?" "It's not that so much Tasha." He swung his valise onto the floor next to him. A perky waitress was immediately on the spot, herself attracted by Jonathon's good looks. They ordered tea and scones and then began conversing in depth about their situation of partner and family matters. She ventured:

"Oh! Jonathon everything is changing so fast. It seemed to me that our days as students were never going to end. I half felt that you and I would never stop our regular coffee dates in the student restaurant. I so enjoyed taking my notes from the lecturers, then meeting you to catch a breath of relaxation and then off to research in the library." Jonathon answered: "Yes it was good earnest enjoyment while it lasted. So many interesting people to meet. But we must face it Jean those days are over now forever. You are leaving for France to au pair within a week or two." "Yes," she replied, "my mother feels it is important for me to see exactly what it means to live and help in a young family. Here!" She slid a slip of paper with an address on it across the table. "You can contact me when you have the opportunity. I know it will be difficult to do this from Sierra Leone. I doubt there will be any stable form of postal system out there."

Jonathon knew that he should contact her when he could so said in answer:

"The first possible time that I can do that is from Cape Town in South Africa when I am on shore leave from the diamond dredging barge off the Orange River mouth later in the year." Jean responded: "Oh! I see! The diamond bearing solid earth gets washed down into the sea."

"Yes," he answered, "there are huge mesh nets and scrapers to drag it all aboard. I have a fairly senior position as someone in control of this. There are local South Africans who will assist me in the somewhat heavy work of getting it all to the sample cabin. But all this must be very boring to you as a young woman." "Not really Jonathon. I am always interested in what you do. Where are you going to stay on leave shifts in Cape Town?" "I am told that boarding house accommodation has been arranged for me," he said.

During the conversation Jean could see that he looked depressed and anxious. Not wanting to upset him further than was necessary she said a little more softly and sympathetically:

"You look worried Jonathon. Is there something bothering you that I don't know about?

Of course I must know everything about you Jon." He glanced sideways embarrassed, but replied tersely:

"Yes there is Jean. It is not only an exciting mission to be going to in this semi third world African state but dangerous too. I have read of constant flare-ups of situations such as civil war and the exploitation of child soldiers. My mother has got to hear about all this and is in a highly nervous state about my going and is upsetting both myself and my father about it. Her protective feelings towards me are being tried to the utmost and I am quite badly distressed by my parents' attitude. They would stop the whole effort of mine if they could."

Jean frowned at the situation that her close friend from student days found himself in. She was not really mature enough in age to comprehend the whole family upset that Jonathon's leaving for Sierra Leone was causing him. Both were only just over twenty one years of age, a time when young people were only just feeling their way into life. Jean said sipping a welcome cup of tea, having risen very early that morning to leave by train to keep their farewell date in London:

"Is there no way out of this Jon?" He replied tensely:

"Unfortunately not Jean. My father of course is wholly in favor of this career for me. I am not like him at all. I am even sleeping badly at the thought of taking the responsibility that I have to in dangerous waters off the West African coast. Because of my qualifications in mining engineering I will have to take charge of a number of men doing dragnet procedures from the seabed there. Actually Jean I am feeling the fear of God in me going into this operation. My mother is just making it worse for me as she was constantly losing her temper and being very short with me that upsets my father. He tried to control the circumstances as he realizes the great future for me financially but my mother does realize the pressure this whole venture is putting on me. Jean was looking most concerned and worried so she responded:

"Yes. From the start of knowing you I could see that you have a very highly strung nature and from what you have told me over the last few years that we have known one another your mother is causing you, if you don't mind me criticizing your family, to make you seem quite unbalanced. Even in your relationships with friends of ours at our past place of study, I could see. I fear for you in how it will all end in this, what I also see as a dangerous and risky situation that is nearly upon you within the next day."

Jonathon banged his elbows deliberately on the table in frustration in doing so nearly spilling their cups of tea. He spat out the words:

"Jean I don't even want to go away now. Seeing your kind placid face across the table from me makes me realize that I never wanted to leave you. You will keep in touch won't you? It seems that I have one anchor in life and that one is you!"

Jean wrinkled her brow earnestly and looked most distressed. That was the reason she liked him so much, exactly the reason, his most obviously sensitive nature. Not only did he look a deep feeling person even though he had been a student of a very manly calling that of geological mining, he was a very touchy person too.

"Jonathon," she said worriedly, "you know you should not have occupied your time in the sciences but in the arts. You would have been much happier." He replied abjectly: "It's not that Jean. It's my family circumstances. On the one hand my mother is in a highly neurotic state about my leaving. On the other side my father although he is as aware as I am of the semi dangerous situation that I am going into, is not showing her a care in the world about it all. I feel trapped between the two.

I do not, even cannot please my mother and throw up my whole future livelihood and that includes you Jean. As far as my father is concerned I just wish he would take a little more interest in what I am going to do. He knows enough about shipboard life from the wartime. At least then I could toughen up as a man to face what's coming to me. I have a nasty feeling that it is going to be one rough ride."

Jonathon glanced at his watch, a waterproof one. He splurted out: "Oh! It has reached the time to leave.

I will need an hour to adjust to the private 'plane trip to Freetown in Sierra Leone. Also there are apparently five or six hardy men who are joining the crew of the diamond mining vessel from Great Britain. I will be working with them so will have to familiarize myself with them even sooner than I thought at this end of the whole scenario."

Jean said sadly:

"Well goodbye for now Jon. You will be in my thoughts for a safe time while you are aboard ship. From what you have told me you are going on after your stint in Sierra Leone, to another mining exploratory area off the South West African coast. You say you will get shore leave in Cape Town?" "Yes," he answered looking anxious. There was not time to tell her of his mother's plans for his romantic future as she, Tasha saw it.

No he would have to write and tell Jean about the ongoing situation as it progressed. He stood up: "Goodbye Jean." He would have like to kiss he, but felt the tearoom too public a place for this gesture, so he just grasped her hand quickly.

Jean watched him walk away then out of the door into the sunny street outside. She thought as she gathered together her handbag and coat so she too could leave: yes, Jonathon is certainly going out into an apparent situation of tropics and palm trees. But civil war was a possibility there. This was something she did not want to be anywhere near. No that was a man's world.

Jonathon had told her what the crew was informed to expect, smouldering tensions from day to day where there were lives of poverty and suspicion against these people who came in from the air and from the sea that caused subdued animosity from them. What did these intruders want from them who were trying to eke out their existence in a seemingly tropical paradise?

Jonathon had told her that he did not need this in his life, being manipulated so and that he was experiencing instability and insecurity anyway from the way he had grown up, especially with his mother's attitude. She was a haughty play actor in her marriage an act she put on continually in her life with her diplomat husband who himself had lived through horrifyingly dangerous experiences during the last world war.

Underneath in her personality Tasha was a product of the scary case histories that she had gone through while nursing the Londoners during the blitz as it had been popularly called at the time. These had been the circumstances of her life while her husband had been fighting from on board the aircraft carriers in the North Atlantic ocean. Tasha was a brave woman but her sharp tongue had upset both her husband and son many times during the marriage.

The superficially peaceful journey to the private airport of London left Jonathon a little calmer after pouring out some of his feelings about job and family to the one person who understood him that was Jean. Where did she say she was going to work? Oh! As an au pair in the French countryside. He thought dimly into their future as he had while a student in his maturing years. This idea of his mother's that he must be acquainted with this girl Marijke who was from a wealthy gold mining family in South Africa was not what he wanted at all in his life.

Great Britain was the place he knew. It meant home and Jean to him. And hadn't his grandfather hinted of an inheritance of the Great House to him in the event of his mother's predeceasing him? Uncannily he thought grimly, not that this was likely. He handed his boarding particulars to the official at the entrance to the small airport. Little did he know it but life as a whole in the big wide world outside was about to begin.

The first sight that came to his eyes was a large sturdy looking aeroplane obviously his means of traveling to Freetown in West Africa. Then he noticed some men in uniform obviously the ones he would have to make himself known to as a member of the company en route to Sierra Leone. But surely he was not the only one leaving.

There was a crowd of people then he noticed milling around a little further off. Standing out from the main throng he could pick out a group of fifteen to twenty men all obviously knowing one another. Jonathon noticed immediately that they looked tough and hardy quite coarse in fact he thought. They were dressed in rough looking clothes clearly ready to do onerous work. They must be part of the crew relay leaving with him by plane from here to do the manual work aboard ship once the 'plane had reached Sierra Leone.

Jonathon for all his geology training felt a spare part when he walked up to the group of crew members he had picked out as the workers aboard the diamond mining barge he would be interacting with. He had been notified that because of his extensive training in mathematical geology he would have a superior position to these men. They all seemed to be in their thirties and forties age wise far older than himself he thought his legs quailing beneath him. He had always been the outsider in the group whether it had been friends or family.

Jean was the only one who had stuck by him socially. He confronted the group of men quite at a loss for what to say. But he need not have worried. There seemed to be one or two more standing out from the others. The atmosphere was tense. One of them said:

"So you are our boss for the contract on ship. You will have to toughen up to face what is coming. There is no need for softies in work like we are going to be doing."

The man had addressed Jonathon slightly maliciously. Jonathon used his wits in the situation as he saw he would have to do in the future. He responded to the taunt:

"Yes I will be accompanying you in the journey and abroad ship."

He knew they did not realize the type of work he would be doing so said:

"I will be doing sea depth tests positioning of the ship in the waters off the coast seabed and dredging up content for geological analysis. Only when we get aboard will we really come to know one another."

Jonathon was now standing close to the small group of ship's crew who would be traveling with him to Freetown in West Africa. As he walked slowly into the group it was obvious to the men that this young man was not some one of their of sort, even though he was a limey. They averted their heads and Jonathon felt their lowered voices and sniggers were directed at him. He knew at once that they were different to himself. He could see they had summed up the fact that although he had been put in charge of them he was a sensitive and intelligent looking person, someone not at all like their own class of rough manual workers.

On a large mining vessel of course people like these were indispensable, for carrying heavy loads of seabed samples, transporting supplies of food and other life sustaining necessities for cooking and generally keeping the ship clean. That the vessel should be kept shipshape was of prime importance for the survival of the men in the dangerous and unpredictable tropical waters off Sierra Leone.

The men were well aware of what they would have to do as a group of workers and had been chosen as such for their muscle and brawn in the situation. They had been on shore leave for six weeks and were now returning to their next sea shift. Jonathon was at a loss to know what to say. He felt the difference of being as chalk to cheese from these people such that his grandfather would have considered mere yokels of no brain. This thought consoled him. So he approached the outskirts of where they were waiting for the `plane that stood close by hoping that they would be told by the officials to go on board for the flight within the next quarter of an hour.

It was obvious to the men that he was chosen as their superior and that he was an intelligent and trained person for the job they were undertaking. Silence fell on the group of men. Were they going to accept this newcomer? He looked a real namby pamby innocent to them as their shifty glances amongst them as crew spoke to them all that words could not.

Jonathan as a man picked up this feeling of slight antagonism towards him and felt he should break the slightly aggressive atmosphere. So he said in a voice not nearly as deep as his crew's:

"Alright men," he asserted himself, "I will be traveling with you to Freetown. Just run through your names." After this relief came as Jonathon spoke. "Oh!

I see we can board the `plane. The Flight Attendant is signaling me. The Company must have given him a description of myself." This statement of his immediately put him one up on the group.

The flight official of the company walked carefully down the steps off the `plane. He had been waiting inside for the time to muster the shift crew but had mainly been watching for Jonathon's arrival. He addressed them all particular Jonathon in saying:

"Good day Mr. Albany and also you men who will be working under him for this six week shift. We are leaving in just over an hour. The pilot and his crews are just freshening up to see that the flight to Freetown is safely directed. This was the beginning of a fairly relaxed few hours ahead amongst the men so they began joking and making ribald comments amongst themselves mainly directed at Jonathon. For what their jobs were worth though they really did want to please their superiors. They were coarsened by reason of the kind of people they had to be in working with tough ironwork, steel netting and heavy implements necessary in the sea mining venture that was beginning with this flight.

The trip was quite a luxury for them and some had brought packs of beer with them to pass the time on the flight. One of the more forward of the main group of men addressed Jonathon in quite a sneaky manner:

"You don't have any nerves about a flight like we are going on?" The others stifled half a laugh and half a snigger. The same man who was the trumped up leader of the group went on more boldly trying in his way to be friendly so that they could all get on especially to ingratiate themselves and please this rather sensitive looking person who would be their boss, in their own way.

It was part of the job. Jonathon looked a bit taken aback as was intended by this as it was obvious to them then. He was quiet for a moment. This was an obvious jibe now that they were aboard and ready to take off from the private airport. Was this the kind of jibing he was going to have to put up with for the next six weeks?

Yes his mother had been right in her over anxious state to say he should see a psychiatrist when he reached South Africa. But she herself was the cause of his over sensitive nature, he knew it he thought grimly to himself as the `plane revved up with a loud roar, something he was not at all used to. There was a loud burst of cheering against the noise of the engine from the shift crew. Jonathon had only flown before in flights to Europe so did not join in the enthusiasm as had learnt once and for all about selfcontrol during his study life.

This private flight in this much smaller aircraft was quite new to him and he tensed a little. The men could see his slight nervousness and out came the beers and jesting and comments began. One of the most forward of the group called Oswald began an attempt at communicating with Jonathon in a nasty and teasing manner. Jonathon sized him up immediately not wanting on the other hand to rise to this bait. Oswald said:

"New to this sort of life are we sir? It's a bit scary at first but we all have learnt to take it. Do you feel that you are in danger sir? Want a beer do you sir? Jonathon was not going to put himself on their level as the person in charge of the crew shift. Then another of them trying to ease the whole journey offered:

"Have a cigarette sir. You'll feel better then.

Jonathon had experienced these sorts of offers before as a student but was not giving in to their whims. He had promised Jean to keep off troublesome addictions. He gave a curt answer:

"No! That is not going to be of any help at all in the long term." He added a little too sharply:

"And it won't do you any good either."

But he knew men and that this sort of thing went on everywhere so after his comment to Oswald he lapsed into silence. He had been hoping to get a glimpse of the Azores the islands in the Atlantic Ocean close by Spain and Portugal and lower down near the coast of Africa. The sea was a mass of blue below and the islands were soon visible as shining emerald jewels passing swiftly below.

Jonathon was enthralled and admitted to himself that it was exciting. As the coast of North Africa came into view his thoughts turned suddenly to his quite frequent consultations with his psychiatrist at his mother's insistence. She did not realize as the doctor had confided to him that it was her over protective nature that had caused this downward spiral of unbalanced thinking and withdrawal in his nature.

Chapter 4

Amid the laughing and talking the beer drinking and the jibes Jonathon's mind was half on what he had been looking at over the ship's rail now magnifying into the vast ocean below. He also dwelt on what he had experienced in his student life and with his grandfather. He was also putting his thoughts onto the psychiatrist who had treated him according to his mother's wishes because he was still under age. He felt that the doctor would like to control his thinking.

Personally he had seen no need for this sort of doctor's handling, but his mother being a nurse considered this sort of treatment as one of the foremost in medical scientific development. As far as Jonathon was concerned it was because of her and her causing his father to be led by the nose that he had been forced into it. As he pondered the situation the ribald jesting of the men traveling with him again seeped into his consciousness. One of the remarks hit home making him angry:

"Now Guv'nor don't be nervous. We aren't."

At this comment sniggers from the others were audible from all around him. The same man persisted:

"Join us in a beer or two then it won't be so hard."

Jonathon slowly turned his head away from the view of the sea below and the approaching north West African coast far in the distance. A thought struck him as he looked. Was that the Sahara desert that he could spot from his `plane seat? Miles and miles of white desert sand receding into the horizon? He had hoped to see something like this he remembered. How he longed for the contract to be over though, and to pursue his post graduate studies in mining geology so he could have Jean's control over his life again.

She was the one gentle soul who understood him. The ribald teasing crept into his thinking once again. How did they know his train of thought at present? Then the leader of the pack Bill riled him again:

"Left a floosie behind hey? That's like all of us. But we don't mind. Gals are two a penny with he-men like us."

At this arrogance Jonathon immediately felt the back of his neck burn with rage with the man's remark. To think they judged him to be like themselves. He raised his head in dignified silence not rising to their insolent jokes. Through the droning sound of the aircraft Jonathon looked up to see the door of the flight cabin opening. The pilot must have told the attendant of the passengers that they were approaching the airport in Sierra Leone. He looked at his watch. He heard the men chuckling with glee. Was he the one they were lampooning with their coarse wit? The leader of the pack chided:

"We've made it Gov'nor. Now the party begins."

Jonathon had a window seat and buckled up to see the landing approach. As they flew lower Jonathon could see from above dark figures dotting the landscape at various places around the makeshift aerodrome. As they came even lower nearly landing on the rough gravel runway he could see that the people in evidence at the landing spot once the `plane had taxied to a stop were wearing much used and dirtied camouflage dresswear.

This caused Jonathon to snap out of his daydreaming about the Great Britain he had just left that was six hours ago. The jesting crew shift member trying to antagonize this man, in his eyes a weak kneed person who was going to be their boss on the trial diamond exploratory ship. Jonathon thought quickly: so this is why the his mother had said she was against this expedition Jonathon had signed up for. A canny man of the crew testing Jonathon seeing his mood change jibed:

"Nervous sir?" Jonathon had to take control. He answered curtly: "Nothing to be afraid of Mr. Forbes. You said that was your name didn't you?" The man immediately cowered knowing his place. He answered: "Just interested Guv'nor. We were all that is us crew members wondering what you felt seeing these army dressed men with guns." Jonathon replied:

"I was warned by the board of directors at the head office of the Company that there has as you so rightly refer to, been a civil war in this African State but that is over for the moment. The head of the employment section of the Company did say this civil war flares up quite often from time to time." "Yes Guv'nor we knew that. It seems part of the job. We are prepared for that. Here we are Guv'nor. Your first time out of Great Britain I'll bet, seeing how green and new to all this that you look."

The ongoing interaction of words directed towards him in the drifting in and out of his consciousness as

leading to civil war that was constantly flaring up in the state.

As these thoughts came to him he though too of Tasha his mother and how she would have felt had she seen what he saw now. That was several jeeps full of rough and undisciplined looking soldiers in camouflage uniforms who drew up to the `plane. There was to Jonathon a stifling tenseness in the atmosphere. These soldiers seemed strangely silent. A strident voice came from behind him:

Don't worry Guv, these men are not going to cause trouble for us. They are just waiting to see that is, if we upset them in any way. They will give us the full treatment if we do," he warned.

Alarmed but not showing it and keeping his facial muscles taut Jonathon said on seeing an empty jeep that had been left ready to take them to the waterfront:

"Let's go then. We need to get to the ship waiting to take us out to the dredging vessel where we will be working for the next six weeks." The leader self instated quipped:

"No need to tell us that Guv'nor." The man added with sudden crestfallenness:

"Only joking sir." He and the crew knew what their jobs were worth.

There was a general scuffle as they all tramped down the steps of the aircraft. The shift crew seemed to know what they were doing and only once on terra firma looked around for their leader Jonathon. What they saw did not inspire much confidence in them. Their spokesman quipped:

"Don't be nervous Guv. It's just a jeep ride down to the small craft to take us out to the dredging barge a little way out to sea. We're ready when you are, Guv. The crew murmured assent trying to be patient while Jonathon, standing at the exit steps tried to take in the situation. What the psychiatrist that his mother as a nurse had put him in touch with had discouraged, was all very real. Yes, the coarseness of the crew's jesting did make him feel not all well equipped to deal with this situation.

His mother's attitude before he had left also did not make him feel much better. She had been entirely against all this in total disagreement with his father, part of whose life in the wartime had been entirely spent in dicey shipboard situations as was coming to them all here. His father had encouraged this "expedition" as his grandfather had called it. These thoughts and experiences that had been just prior to leaving including his goodbyes to Jean flashed through his mind as did his testing in geological sciences that he had undergone in his studies. The outspoken member of the crew jibed:

"Face it Guv'nor. This is for real. You are the one who has got to tell us all about the dredging aboard the "Glasgow Star." "The name of the ship entered vaguely into his consciousness as he jumped agily into the jeep. With cowered suspicious faces the jeep-fulls of other soldiers here and there parked around the landing strip of the makeshift landing strip stared at these arrivals. They had been told of the possible wealth in alluvial diamond minerals being washed out to sea and lying on the sea bed.

Palm trees dotted the jungle leading down to the sea that lay far off as they could see. But all this tropical paradise did not seem important to the men. The survival instinct made them laugh grimly in the back of the jeep that spluttered into action. They were off. The ill-cared for vehicle swung from side to side. The men were thrown one against another. Jonathan had summed up the situation to come with his eyes sweeping the road as he had seen when leaving the aircraft.

He had let the shift crew onto the jeep and had himself at least a crouched position at the truck's rear holding onto the back while the driver steered a jolting and uncomfortable ride, half of it through what Jonathon now was fully aware was jungle territory. It was so unpleasant that he let his thoughts drift back into his experiences with his grandfather during his stay at the Great House back in Britain.

The old man like his parents played on his nerves. Yes they had understood that he wanted to get qualified and to have a job. But why had they all been so against this one? This reason of theirs he began to realize, as it was getting more and more unpleasant in the truck although his young body tolerated it. His mother's voice came into his subconscious:

"Jonathon you are involving yourself in something that for someone as sensitive as yourself is going to be impossible to handle. I foresee disaster coming out of this activity. Please let it be forgotten about, leave it alone. Rather further you studies and find a land based job." Then his father's voice interrupted in these words of his mother's, creating conflict and confusion in his mind:

"Son shipboard life as I know it from World War 2 is total discomfort. Severe discipline and organization is necessary, but character forming."

Jonathon recalled how he had sulked out a reply to them both, needing at the time to speak to his psychiatrist:

"It's all that I could find advertised in the newspaper to earn my living." Then Tasha had said impatiently while smoking as he had noticed that she often did:

"Jonathon we will condone your decision to work on the diamond mining dredger off the West African coast but please darling do all you can to keep yourself safe."

Then he looked around him getting to grips with reality and saw the jungle territory receding as the truck reached a very unsteady looking wooden jetty on the side of a river that was flowing into the sea. This was where the diamond bearing silt was washed onto the seabed that he and the team were going to investigate.

Jonathon realized with a shock that this risky situation was what Tasha had meant him to negotiate carefully. He raised his eyes to see the end of the mission ahead the diamond exploratory barge. Squinting into the distance he could see the ship their destination lying far out.

Jonathon's thoughts as a qualified geologist swung from his studies to his parents and psychiatrist and then into the present. Why had Tasha been so against him leaving Great Britain? She was a nurse someone who understood why if it was a young man, someone would want to get into and try this risky situation.

He fought against her in his thoughts just as he had when he had been with her and Grant his grandfather, towards the departure from the Great House. Playing it up in us mind his psychiatrist's words hit into his consciousness. The doctor had said:

"Are you trying your mother's nerves Jonathon? Are you doing this on purpose to make her loosen her apron strings from you that she should let you go your own way?"

As the boat splashed through the seawaters of the tropics out to the diamond dredging ship out at sea the responsibility he held in this situation played on his mind. His mother was continually carping against his father's smoking. It this was constantly getting on Jonathon's nerves. He recalled momentarily that the psychiatrist had asked him how he usually reacted to his parents' interplay with each other and himself in the family's communication. Jonathon could hear himself answering:

"It's not that I hate my parents. It's just that my father had a nervewracking time in the aircraft carriers on the North Atlantic Ocean in the wartime. My father was a constant bundle of nerves for this reason, and was constantly losing his temper because of it. I tried in vain to understand the situation but because I also intended to make shipboard life my employment future I developed his sense of basic fear about this."

Jonathon looked around him and out towards their destination the large ship looming ever closer. He tried to clear his mind of the place and occurences he had left. This was exciting. The dredger was soon leaning above them. The shift crew were quiet. They knew they would have to make a dangerous rope lift onto the larger vessel. As the small craft filled with its passengers the shift crew became terse and tight-lipped. The motor of the largish boat that would carry them out to the mining vessel further out to sea broke the silence of the mid tropical day in what could have been a holiday paradise. That was except for the armed soldiers who had welcomed them, Jonathon thought grimly. It appeared to him that the group was leaving one possible danger, one for another out at sea.

From what he could see as the small boat carrying them all drew nearer the experimental diamond mining barge the vessel that would shelter them looked worn and in need of repair. The paintwork over the black iron sides he could see was looking weather beaten. In trepidation he wondered what it would be like on board.

The small craft drew up to the side of the anchored ship. The men were tight lipped now. They knew that their six week work shift had begun. Jonathon on looking upwards could see another group of men waiting to help them aboard. It seemed that their personal effects would be swung up by hoist, and the relieving crew would have to climb what at least was a sturdy looking thickly knotted rope ladder that had been thrown down to them.

As the person with seniority Jonathon held back while the crew ascended one by one at a shout from above. Then Jonathon was left alone in the motorboat with only the driver of the vessel. He hesitated, new to this sort of thing. The driver said:

"Go on up now. It's your turn. I can't wait much longer as the tide is turning and I don't want to knock the big ship if the wind gets up."

The hoist came down again. Jonathon put his pack onto his back and grasped the first rung of the ladder. The rope was tough and scraped at his hands. He was young and fit though and was soon climbing carefully upwards trying not to look at the frightening depths below. The weather was hot and steamy and he had built up a sweat as he reached the deck of the mining barge. A voice greeted him as he climbed over the railings of the ship. The man who spoke was clearly the captain of the great vessel as he began talking with a note of authority:

"You must be our mining engineer. We have held up all dredging activities for the few days that we have been anchored here. We were notified by radio that you and the shift crew would be arriving today. Welcome aboard."

Jonathon tried to look manly and important at the man's words but inside he was quaking with the fear of the situation that Tasha had put into him. Her fright with Jonathon's leaving to undertake this job had left him very disillusioned. He tried to muster up the appropriate reply to the captain. He was quiet for a few moments in the seaman's presence. He realized with a start that he and the rest of the shift would have to tolerate one another's company in an all male situation for the next six weeks. The captain introduced himself:

"I am Captain Boyd. We have anchored here off the coast of Sierra Leone having sailed out from Southampton under the auspices and direction of the diamond mining company. We were expecting you at anytime in the last forty-eight hours because as I can tell you Mr. Albany—you are Mr. Jonathon Albany is it not so?—that this is a most unreliable and dangerous country to be in. We have all our food and other supplies necessary stocked in the hold of the ship. The executives of the Company gave binoculars to me and I have been studying from this ship what I can see from here on the coast that you have just left. Am I right, Mr. Albany that there are child soldiers on the loose inland? You and the crew have just left there to come aboard here. I do not envy what you have just come from if this is so."

Jonathon was sure now that the Captain meant well. He had not felt because he was still a young man, any sense of fear at the rifle armed men and boys in camouflage suits who had been making their presence felt at the crumbling airstrip where he and the shift crew had arrived. Perhaps this was what his mother had been nearly hysterical about when she had heard about the job that he was undertaking. He knew she followed the newspapers.

His consciousness about the ongoing situation flared in his mind. He would apparently have to have a few words with this man.

He wondered in his capacity of being a geological mining engineer supervising diamond exploration on the seabed where they were anchored whether he or the captain were the more sensitive about the undertaking and bearing the brunt of what was involved. Inwardly he quaked at the situation and decided to give this somewhat older man the benefit of the doubt in the question of who would take the most responsibility at sea for the safety of the crew on board. So he spoke:

"I found no danger at the time we all landed in the capitol of Freetown. The only thing that I did experience was a strong atmosphere of tension and suspicion. I suppose the people who are indigenous to Sierra Leone are dependant on not being disturbed in their day to day living."

The Captain agreed and the conversation drifted on as the two men sized one another up. Finally Captain Boyd on seeing a passing seaman summoned him to take Jonathon to his quarters that turned out to be a single cabin. Lunch was apparently also at hand. In the cabin close to the sorting dredge workroom everything around him looked clean but drab. It seemed as if there was going to be nothing exciting about all this.

He changed and prepared for sleep having been told by Captain Boyd that there would be an officer to show him the basic routines aboard, and the navigation room where he would be working some of the time in the shifting position of the ship according to what was pulled up from the seabed by the dredging team. Jonathon tried to adjust as he fell asleep Jean's face was in his mind. Why did they have to be separated? That was what Tasha had said.

Why was it necessary to go so far away to have even studied the geological formation of the earth's crust. What a bore. But for a young man it was exciting as the board of directors had told him that it would be. So far so good. He had experienced a sense of fear at the rumbling jeeps full of soldiers with rifles, but no one else had seemed to be worried.

All fell quiet except for an odd creaking of the ship's iron plates and timbers and the lapping of seawater against the vessel. The next thing Jonathon experienced was a knock on the cabin door. A roughly dressed young man with a work hardened face spoke to him as he saw Jonathon waking. The ship rolled from to time and Jonathon sprang out of bed saying:

"Am I late?" The steward replied: "No sir. I called here in good time for breakfast as Captain Boyd ordered. I will just wait until you have washed and changed." Jonathon enquired saying: "You will show me the navigation room and the dredging sample room then?" The man looked ready to help and said again: "I'll hand you over to Captain Boyd once you are ready. He has been up and about for some time now."

Jonathon presumed from this that he some sort of rank as a geological officer on board the ship. A lean breakfast was served in the dining cabin. The rolling of the ship did not improve his appetite he was finding. The captain then loomed large in Jonathon's presence approaching him as he rose. He said:

"Good morning Mr. Albany. We will have a full day together to go over the ship's routines and movements as far as you and I are concerned. We will be in charge of the dredging as I am sure you will be aware concerning the pulling up of seabed sediment and its thorough examination for diamond bearing content. The other area of your work aboard is to work with our navigation steering officer in the slight movement of the location of the ship according to what is dredged up. This will happen every few days."

The Captain stood back while Jonathon scrutinized some of the navigational paperwork to do with the positioning of the ship, and marine calculations as to the current depth of the ocean that had been made in the last few days. To start off the day on a professional note Jonathon inquired:

"Captain Boyd could you state quite bluntly if there has indeed been the routine daily dredging, as I have been informed of by the company's representatives before I left? Can you tell me if so far there has been any diamond bearing sediment in what has been pulled up from the ocean bed within the last few days?" Captain Boyd was immediately cooperative and answered:

"It is difficult to sight a spot where we consider the richest diamond bearing material is lying on the ocean's bed. This would have been washed down stream in the river. This is a stream flowing from the geologically rich diamond deposit area inland that has been discovered at the source that is being washed into the sea."

Jonathon immediately understood his role in the situation. It would be up to his mathematical knowledge now to advise from samples pulled up from the ocean what were the properties of salt and fresh water where the ship should be lying. This would be so as to anchor in the best possible position to dredge up possible diamond mineral bearing samples. He replied to Captain Boyd:

"That has clarified everything. I can begin liaising with the crew immediately. I am sure they are up and about by now this morning." The captain said again: "I have been informed by the ship's radio officer that there has been a message through from headquarters that we are to keep them informed. You will have to undertake to send statistics through to them regularly about what we find in examining the seabed samples coming up on board in the daily dredging operations."

Jonathon and the captain were standing on an open space on deck. There were several crewmembers manning the dredging hoists. With his mathematical and geological knowledge Jonathon immediately slotted into the situation. He noticed that there were three groups of men. It was apparent that seawater and ocean bed sediment were being pulled up.

Jonathon and the captain approached each group one by one and introductions were made and pleasantries exchanged. Jonathon addressed one of the groups at random:

"Are you bearing up in this humid weather?" The morning was heating up. The ship was anchored in tropical waters and Jonathon had yesterday with the landing of the `plane experienced something of the discomfort of the midday sun. He realized this was what was to be expected during the six weeks that he was due to be aboard. A spokesman answered:

"Yes sir." The group that he was becoming acquainted with were grim in their response to their new officer's query. Captain Boyd had just made it known to the men that Jonathon was their superior. A spokesman of the dredging crew said, disregarding what he considered a dig at the men's self control in the heat:

"We will be bringing samples through to the dredging laboratory from time to time as soon as we can. Then it is over to you and the lab assistants to analyze the material and sea water content." At this Captain Boyd put in:

"Yes Mr. Albany. We need to be aware of the amount of fresh water from the river flowing down from the interior into the sea:"

Jonathon picked up the strain of thinking and verbal interplay into what his role in the procedure was and quickly responded:

"Yes I'm sure we'll have to examine scientifically the relative amount of sea water and fresh water where the ship lies of the coast. The company has already informed me that this is necessary for the positioning and anchoring of the vessel so as to get the best anchorage for the dredging. This is so as to note the navigation officer's decision as to the best spots ultimately to mine the ocean bed." Dryly the captain added to this:

"Of course the best mining positions for the ship are changing all the time. I can tell you that from experience Mr. Albany. Everything changes constantly at sea."

Not to be outdone by this male vying for authority Jonathon responded:

"Everything is constantly changing on land too." He wondered briefly to himself in saying this if it was Tasha his mother's influence on his thinking. She had made it quite clear to him that she did not like his being at sea. Captain Boyd spoke again:

"We'll just have a quick look into the dredging analyzing quarters and then lunch will be served. The sea air, humid as it is gives one a hearty appetite. Then we can visit the radio cabin."

Lunch as Captain Boyd had mentioned was a silent but necessary enjoyment for the men, all officers in Jonathon's situation. It was becoming clear to him that although he did not have any clear navigational duties he was by reason of his student qualifications to be regarded as a senior person aboard, that the Captain had told him. After lunch was over Captain Boyd sensing his feeling, said:

"Don't concern yourself with the somewhat ignorant attitude of the crew aboard here. I myself have a difficult time handling their duties, delegating haulage out of the seabed, movement of the ship according to what is hoisted up with regard to our main purpose here, that is the mining of diamond bearing matter."

Jonathon was feeling a little relieved at these words as he was very young in comparison to the men who were crewing aboard with him. He queried:

"What have I got to have to do with them sir?" The Captain answered as he opened the door of the radio room where the two of them were headed:

"Very little my lad. The ship's officers keep the lower ranks under good control. The tropical heat gets us all down as you would imagine."

It was getting on for the middle of the day and Jonathon did indeed feel more and more uncomfortable. Curious now about what the Captain was showing him once they were inside the radio cabin he could see before him there a panel of what seemed very up to date machinery with dials and numbers all ticking away noisily with static from time to time.

He thought to himself: how was he ever going to assimilate all this? Captain Boyd seeing his more than slight nervousness spoke:

"Yes, this is all part of what we are proceeding with aboard here in the search for diamond bearing sea bed crust that has been lying on the ocean bed, having as has been discovered by the company's miners, washed down from the source some way up river inland from the coast."

Captain Boyd then began the explanation of the dial parts. Gradually what Jonathon had studied mathematically at university in Scotland began to make sense to him in Captain Boyd's words of saying what was ongoing in the ship's purposes where they were anchored.

CHAPTER 5

At last as the tropical heat came to a climax on Jonathon's first day aboard the diamond dredger it became a little clearer of what his role was to be aboard. The captain spoke from time to time as Jonathon studied the dials and numbers and indicators in the front of the cabin. His electronic and mathematical knowledge made it clear to him how the data from the radio and sounding records worked to indicate position, depth and direction of the movement of the dredger.

Through his concentration after a while the captain who was curious of Jonathon's part in the capacity he was employed in aboard said:

"I don't want to interrupt but would just like to say that if you have any trouble with the crew please let me know. They are a rough though golden hearted lot. I am just surmising that they might take advantage of you by unpleasant teasing when they realize the seniority you have here even though you are obviously to all a very new and green person. I have already spoken to them about the rank you hold here even though we do not wear uniform on a ship of this type." Jonathon answered:

"Thank you captain. Yes you have picked up quite correctly that I am more than just nervous in this situation. I know my stuff yes about the seabed and seawater analysis but am quite exposed when as you say these men see how young I am. From what I can make out they do seem a very rough but hale and hearty group of men.

I am sure they mean well. The only thing I will not take to is any teasing and wasting of my time. They can do it amongst themselves, yes but I wish to be left out of anything like that. For a start it is not my class to consort with people like that on their level." "Understood," said the captain. "I will monitor the group carefully for any show of familiarity towards you. You will mostly be talking with them through the officers junior to me. I am expecting a couple of them here within a few minutes. Jonathon again put his mind to the interpretation of the radio works that were humming and buzzing with activity. Suddenly some of the static became louder than usual traveling over the airwaves.

Jonathon was unperturbed at first because from what he could see of what happened in this radio room with his technical knowledge of such equipment, this was constantly going on. There was a continual buzzing and squeaking coming through as the dials and numbers changed on what he could see several screens. He tried to tie all this up in his mind with what he had disciplined himself in while studying in Scotland. The captain however who obviously had some knowledge of all this pulled himself up and said after Jonathon had been trying to take all this into his mind while communicating his findings verbally with Captain Boyd, in a pause in the conversation said:

"There is a message coming through from head office. This is entirely unexpected at this time."

Jonathon tried to focus on where the Captain was indicating on the mass of radio equipment. The Captain seeing that Jonathon was not going to make a move at trying to get the message on the air that was persistently coming through from head office realized that this was an unusual attempt at trying to get through on the ship's radio equipment. at this time of day. He said again:

"It is apparently a woman's voice coming through on the radio wave band connected to this ship's radio room."

Still quite unconcerned not at all expecting that this was someone who wanted his own attention, Jonathon said pointedly in the situation:

"I wouldn't have thought that women were involved in this kind of work Captain. What is the connection with us at this moment?" Captain Boyd was putting his ear to the message trying to make some sense of what was coming through on the radio. The static resolved into a gratingly high squeak and a woman's voice became clearer and then to his horror the voice became finally recognizable. It was Tasha his mother. Then slowly as the moments ticked by on the clock at the top of the panel it became clear that not only was the radio two way connection very piercing in sound to both the captain's ears but also to his own hearing. Tasha's voice was clearly quite hysterical as well as he picked up audibly what she was saying:

"Jonathon? Jonathon? Are you there? You must be!" She repeated her words three of four times. Then Jonathon took control of the situation. Two other very masculine looking officers in the radio room with them were looking most annoyed. This was becoming embarrassing to Jonathon. What did his mother want? This was typical of her interference in his life.

Jonathon's thoughts began to gather momentum as he started to focus on what his mother was trying to put across the airwaves to him, her son. The captain was bending over the radio dials in a most uncomfortable posture but said with considerable self control:

"It seems to be a woman who is trying to speak to you Mr. Albany." Jonathon said as amiably as he could with all the other static coming through:

"Yes I am aware now that it is my mother. I do apologize sir for this inconvenience. It seems she needs to speak to me. She seems almost hysterical. I will try and calm her when she hears my voice." The captain answered:

"Here is the voice transmitter where you can come through to her."

Did Jonathon imagine it or was the captain showing a half smirk on his face at this unseemly interruption to the daily procedure of the exploratory mining vessel anchored off the coast. Jonathon shrugged this off in his communication with the captain and tried to concentrate on what his mother was saying. He heard her words:

"Jonathon I am nearly going out of my mind worrying about your safety in this sea mining venture you are involved in. Why are you doing this? Surely there are one hundred and one land mining operations you can employ yourself in. I am following the news about West Africa. These countries are most unstable and civil war can flare up at any time in these places Jonathon. You have no military training. How are you going to survive in this awful contract? I warned you not to sign yourself into anything like this."

Jonathon could hear his mother now and was feeling a little paranoid in the situation because the Captain and the other two officers in the cabin were beginning to be restless and embarrassed at the interruption to their duties. From what they could here this woman speaking to Jonathon was sounding uncontrolled and desperate. Again a high-pitched voice came through to the cabin:

"Jonathon! Jonathon? Are you there? Answer me please."

Slowly as was his reaction to this Jonathon spoke into the radio sharply:

"Mother you must control yourself. I am busy at work aboard ship and the officers here are most put out at being interrupted by domestic matters. You must not interfere with what I am doing here."

Tasha began to let out a stream of words from what Jonathon could glean. She was nearly distraught with worry about his safety. As she ranted on he caught the main gist of what she was trying to get through to her son. She repeated over and over:

"I am constantly reading in the newspapers about civil war igniting in the West African states. They are highly unstable. Do you realize the danger you are in?" Jonathon began to feel uneasy with a creeping paranoia at her ranting and raving in full hearing of the officers in the navigating room. It was obvious to Jonathon that his mother's voice was interrupting the routine of the morning.

Jonathon could not just shut off the dial bringing her voice through to the control cabin. He put a stony expression onto his face, hiding his feelings as Tasha's voice continued irritatingly over the radio static. Jonathon turned to apologize to the officers with him. The Captain he could see had a faint smile around his face. The man said:

"Let her finish. Perhaps if you could get a word in to pacify her to some small extent she will realize that all is under control here both on board ship and in the country inland. Jonathon took him at his word. There was a pause in the high and hysterical woman's voice over the static. Then Tasha came through with a final thrust of words:

"Jonathon? Jonathon? Can you hear me?" Jonathon took his chance to try and pacify her in what was developing into a somewhat awkward situation in the radio cabin. He drew closer to the mouthpiece on the radio set and spoke firmly:

"Mother? Mother! Can you hear me? A cowed voice at having finally received a communication from her son came over the airwaves:

"Jonathon you must do everything you can to keep safe. I am hearing about frightful atrocities happening in the West African States. Is this going on where you are?"

Jonathon who had not experienced any violence in his transportation through the jungle territory so far to the mining ship took a deep breath and answered as soothingly as he could:

"Mother Are you still there?" What seemed to be a sigh of relief coupled with more static came through. He heard a faint: "Yes Jonathon. Please tell me you are alright!" Jonathon took his cue:

"Mother all that I could see when the `plane landed were some men who were armed, yes but there was no fighting, clashes or violence. We are going ashore again both to monitor the diamond bearing source of the river that washes the alluvial bearing soil into the sea and also to stock up supplies of food for supplies on board.

The day settled as Tasha went off the air and the afternoon drew on although Jonathon like the rest of the crew was feeling uncomfortable in the near equatorial heat. It was difficult to concentrate at first but he took in what an average day's routine would include mostly liaising with the crew he had already met while flying into Freetown. At the time Tasha had finished speaking to her son he was feeling quite uneasy at her words, indeed somewhat paranoid.

The Captain and two senior officers he imagined were glancing at him and one another in what seemed to him to be a kind of mocking way. Were they harping on his youth and innocence as well as his inexperience? They as well as the crew? He thought grimly, yes he was in for a difficult time if so. But surely he was a well qualified person for the job. The sense of unease gradually wore off when the reality of the Captain's voice filtered into his consciousness:

"We will be doing the usual depth soundings and dredging of ocean bed content. This is where we will need you to work with our navigating officers to find an accurate ocean anchorage for the ship directly linking up to the direction that the river is flowing into the sea here. We have been doing a certain amount of sorting of seabed content but need to take an clear reading of the ship's position so as to draw up samples most likely to contain diamond bearing sediment."

Gradually the worry and persecution of Tasha's voice lifted off Jonathon's mind. This was becoming interesting therefore he responded with what he considered an intelligent question:

"So I will have a lot to do with the dredgers tomorrow sir?" The Captain looked at the officer and said:

"The crew will be up at the usual time tomorrow?" Clearly Captain Boyd wanted to have the best possible relationships for all on board. This simple question drew Jonathon into the future proceedings on the ship. The officer answered:

"Yes. Mr. Albany, we are usually ready to start work at about nine in the morning. There is a cheerful bonhomie amongst the crew who are very willing. Any camaraderie or teasing I would take with a pinch of salt. What they say is generally kindly meant."

Jonathon thought to himself: was he reading too much into all this? Captain Boyd had a smile on his face in the speaking of these words but went on to say:

"Some time as the week pans out we will be making a shore party inland to Freetown to scout for extra food supplies expected to be ferried in by air. Also we have been asked by the company to check to digging operations inland where there is, and I say this confidentially definitely diamond bearing material."

After rising the crew already aboard faced what was for them another monotonous day. Jonathon as a relative newcomer was a little more keyed up at the new surroundings by now. The heat drew in as the day progressed. He was by now used to the swaying and stomach churning caused by the ship. He stood, cynical now about the almost constant bonhomie of the dragnet men preparing for operations down below in the seabed off their vessel. He pulled himself up though.

There was work to do and he would have to liaise with the crew. He walked over to the men on deck. He felt an immediate tension. They had all to get to know what he would be like to work with. Jonathon began to feel the strain as the first couple of hours ticked by. He had made his salutations to the officers and more important it seemed, to the Captain. He eased himself into the group there totally conscious of his unique position as calculating marine mathematician that he had studied for.

He took up his equipment and having finished with the morning's pleasantries he climbed down the steps backwards again to work in positioning and sounding the depths with the crew. It was clear that although not much was required of him the men were becoming somewhat physically worked out as the day wore on towards the generally welcomed lunch break. Much plumbing and largely trial runs ensued during the day. At first he had asked:

"Are we due for taking up samples today from the ocean bed?"

At this the crew as a whole had looked sulky and uncommunicative. Jonathon was feeling increasingly awkward as the tropical heat discomforted all aboard. Finally he got an answer from the leader a rather more jovial and hearty individual than the rest of them. This man also seemed to know more about what had to be done as far as Jonathon was concerned. He spoke a little tersely for all this that Jonathon was feeling:

"Come to this gap in the rails sir and we'll do a drop together."

Jonathon immediately tensed at the man's voice

The week did not as Jonathon had hoped when rising from his cabin bed the first morning on the dredger ship, mean that the hours and minutes sped by. The work seemed to involve heavy and patience demanding effort. He found it necessary constantly to be at the beck and call of the crew that were actually pulling up the samples and plummeting the depths below the ship's rail.

He was also needed in the ship's navigation room for repositioning of the vessel according to what encrustations were being lifted up from the ocean bed by the crewmen. Suddenly it all seemed very boring and uncomfortable despite the heat that made the situation even worse. Was this all going to go on forever? Despite his quick brain concerned with the mathematical calculations he had been trained for as a student that he needed to have to do his part in the work the men and he were all doing together he began to miss Jean.

His mind blurred slightly from time to time as the odd idle moment crept into his thinking while the men pulled up the sand coated samples. He thought of Jean. She must have reached France by now and settled in with the family that she was going to au pair for and care for. His mind also jumped into the future. His natural instinct made him almost jealous of the situation that she as his committed girlfriend was living in.

Suddenly one of the crew's words forced its way into his consciousness. Tersely he became aware that the present wait for the current sample was making him drift away in his concentration on the job. Irritatingly one of the men was saying:

"Are we right for this pull-up sir? Jody and I are waiting for your confirmation in the recording of this drop."

Jonathon was confused. His thoughts were on Jean and even further deep down in his thinking his mother's whole attitude to this venture. She was having the effect of making him extremely nervous. Tasha had been so confident in imparting to him that he must, must meet this girl Marijke when he reached Cape Town as was part of his contract. How would Jean react to this when he wrote to her about it? It was not fair on her.

"Sir," the man's voice cut into his drifting thoughts, "we need you now to tell us the calculation result for the plumb line drop we have to do now."

Off and on during the days over the next week the activities of the men became routine. They were just moving shapes in Jonathon's sight. He could see them all and they spoke to him yes, but perhaps it was their personal thinking that he could not get to grips with. That was it he thought. None of these people could ever any of them be a friend to him. To test this principle he had arrived at into communication with the crew he spoke, tensely as they all did in the tropical heat.

"Bill when did Capptain Boyd say that we were going on a shore party?" The man answered shrewdly:

"It is no use thinking it will be any less comfortable ashore in these parts. I have been on shore leave to the alluvial investigating works inland. The road leading there is a disaster and the jungle gets ever more thick as the jeep takes you inland. Oh! Now you mention it Jon . . ." the man used his nickname—how did he know his school and study mates who had been closer to him personally had used this way of addressing him? It was an uncomfortable feeling. The man who was obviously most popular amongst the ones Jonathon was working him, was clearly like the rest of the men a little in awe of this young man. This person a young man senior to them was definitely a classy pommey brainbox as far as they were concerned. He did not seem to give them any nonsense though so he was tolerated amongst them all. The man finished his little splab about what to expect inland firstly by saying:

"It'll be no use telling the Captain that you don't want to go with us to scrape out samples of earth in the inland mining area, everyone has to go. Only a skeleton crew is left aboard at these times."

Jonathon tensed again at Bill's words wondering if the man was trying to get the upper hand again. Did he consider him slightly useless just because he did not lift and shift the heavy mining gear like the rest of them? Was he different to the others? It was such questions and doubts that he had had all his young life so far. He was a clever intelligent person yes, he knew but it just didn't seem to go down with such as these folk.

Bill finished the morning's work by saying to Jonathon in a jumped up fashion:

"There'll be a meeting tomorrow for shore leave arrangements and we'll be off in the motor boat mid morning." It felt to Jonathon that this man wanted to be in control. But that was his job he angered himself in his thoughts.

As the leader of the rough crew hands had predicted the shore party when it did transpire the next day was even more uncomfortable than the steady seabed operations of plumbing the ocean depths at irregular intervals during the days had been. The tropical salty air seemed to cause a stickiness of salt residue all over the men's bodies.

The only positive thing about the trip so far was that the crew and senior men were at least by now accustomed to the swaying and rolling of the mining vessel out at sea off the coast of Sierra Leone. Then it was change of mode again for the crew. A load hailer summoned them all to the gap in the ship's rail where the motorboat was waiting below. Jonathon tried to look as if he were one of the group aboard who were not involved in this mission but in passing the captain, this senior officer spoke meaningfully to the young man and though he kept the relationship jovial he said:

"Now young man I know this is a sea mining investigatory project by the company but I have been informed by radio by the chief executive that you with your high qualifications will be indispensable in the goal of testing the old mining dump ashore. We wish to take geological samples to compare and see if it can be established that the river that has its source in the area inland is indeed washing alluvial soil into the sea and in what direction once it reaches the estuary. That is where the fresh water from the river meets the salt ocean water."

All this was of course quite obvious to Jonathon who responded a little glumly at being roped in to join the little party.

"Right you are sr. Can you give me a quick run down as to the exact equipment that I will need to take with me to conduct my geological experiments?"

Captain Boyd looked a bit annoyed at these words but said tactfully:

"Surely you know what instruments are necessary for the job?" Jonathon quailed slightly at this semi-reprimand

After an hour or so that morning the Captain finally mustered the shore party down into the motorboat and then amidst slightly nervous behavior they disembarked at the very defunct jetty. There were a couple of uniformed locals to meet them. As Jonathon watched the motorboat recede into the distance back to the anchored vessel out at sea he began to feel very isolated and nervous.

The uniformed men hustled the crew who had arrived into a decrepit old truck and after much chugging and revving up they were on their way down a horribly bumpy road, uneven and full of stones in the way. The road merged into very jungly territory. Jonathon was feeling most uncomfortable because the jerking of the truck threw the men's bodies one against the other. When not coping with the situation on the back of the vehicle all thrown together, Jonathon caught glimpses through the trees of dark figures in camouflage uniforms carrying what seemed to him like dangerous weapons. The situation was tense.

As they progressed one or two other trucks passed by carrying more armed men some of them looking no more than twelve years of age who had been rounded up by their driver. The palm trees at the side of the river by the side of the beach were no more and the gravel road entered into thick jungle. The leader of the rough shore leave crew quipped nervously:

"Do you think we are ever going to get out of here alive?" The men mumbled and then spoke sharply to one another in fright and anticipation. One of them said:

"Does anyone know where we are heading to or why we have to do this trip?" Another of them looking for a scapegoat in the highly isolated and what seemed dangerous situation they were in addressed Jonathon aggressively:

"Yes! You are the one reason that we have had to take this trip. We others are not really necessary. The company has forced us to accompany you because of these devils who live here who could threaten or attack the whole lot of us. Jonathon felt his face pale. Thoughts of Tasha and Jean flashed through his brain. Hadn't Tasha his mother been right about the idiocy of undertaking this African expedition? They began to see apes, giant monkeys swinging through the trees. One or two of these animals latched onto the now grinding forward movement of the truck. One of the apes snatched at some of their food supplies for the journey. The men were astounded and grabbed helplessly at their provisions but to no effect.

The whole trip inland became gradually a burdensome task. The jungle ended and a derelict town came into view. They passed through it slowly with tattered locals trying to halt them begging for food. They drove through uneventfully and then arrived at the mine diggings near the slow source of the river. Unenthusiastically because of the heat the men took hold of their sample containers. A couple of shabby looking inhabitants sulkily affirmed their arrival by letting the truck carrying the men into a fenced in area.

Slowly the men got to work and the containers were filled. Halfheartedly in the heat of the day as it approached noon Jonathon halted the proceedings saying:

"I think we have enough earth samples to go on with. Nothing seems to be going on here. I was told that the Sierra Leone Government was investigating for possible alluvial finds, but everything just seems to be going to waste." Bill muttered amongst the men:

"Typical! These people don't know a good thing when it is right under their noses."

As the early afternoon clamped down the men already suffering from heat fatigue loaded the truck and bad temperedly now took the journey back to the beach where the motor boat lay waiting. The men exhausted now finished off the day by washing and eating.

Day followed day for another two weeks and then another meeting was called. It was apparent that Jonathon and three or four chosen others were to be flown out from the capital Freetown's airport, down through to the Democratic Republic of Congo to Cape Town in South Africa.

There he would await further instructions to join a diamond mining barge off the Orange River mouth where rich alluvial deposits lay on the seabed. These had been washed slowly down river into the ocean from the inland town of Kimberley. Jonathon recalled this as being internationally famous for its diamond wealth in the area. Jonathon received this news gladly as the heat was getting him down.

Slowly and gradually the whole purpose of what the company was aiming at and his own part in it filtered into Jonathon's mind. Off and on his thinking flashed back to his mother and father and more often to Jean. Tasha his mother and his ties to her were becoming a hindrance in his life aboard ship. She was the one who was causing him to take a negative attitude to what he was doing although the tasks assigned to him were easy enough with his intelligence.

Again a meeting was called. The men who would be leaving Freetown that included Jonathon sat in a group in the navigation cabin waiting to be addressed by the captain. Bill the leader of the pack as usual stirred up his workmates' thinking and feelings. He spoke looking around him:

"Just as well it's still early. Don't you men find it more difficult to keep the tussle of work going when the heat sets in? At least we don't have to sit in a sweat here. It's still early. Has anyone got the time?"

Another support of Bill's breaking the ice so to speak for the group meeting said:

"Just on nine now."

Jonathon who had adjusted somewhat in the crew's combined activities abroad joined in:

"I don't think the captain will be long now."

As he spoke the one referred to opened the cabin door and walked briskly in and greeted the crew waiting for him:

"Greetings and good morning men. Just let me be seated and take out the notes of instruction that I worked on late last night. Yes. Here we are. Six of you that is including you Mr. Albany"—he looked directly at Jonathon, "will be flying out within the next few days via the Democratic Republic of Congo and Angola, to the company's headquarters in Cape Town to find lodgings and await further instructions there. That will be to join with a politically sensitive—I am warning you men about this—group of workers from South Africa.

The country there is in a state of political upheaval at the moment and I have been asked to let you men be aware and tactful of the feelings of the new group who will be working with you. I have been asked by the company that you realize that we do not want trouble politically speaking. You all know already that the British are accepted and well liked all over the world. South Africa has been unpopular for decades now because of its politics of inequality. You must know what I mean."

A murmur of disgruntled affirmation at the captain's words ran around the group. The men all of them had become used to a certain routine on board. In spite of their somewhat aching limbs because of the physical nature of their work walking to and fro with containers of samples and activating mechanical devices bending and stretching, this had made them all more than ready for deep sleep on the ship that swayed up and down on the sucking of the ocean swells. Now apparently this was going to change. The captain addressed the men again:

"I am going to read out the names of the men who will be returning to Great Britain and the ones who will be continuing in the work of alluvial exploration down south in Africa." Bill quipped:

"Did we get anything done in finding diamond bearing sea sand from below?" He looked pointedly at Jonathon and said with a mean tone to his voice:

"He's the one. He should know. What's he doing on board with us if he can't tell us of anything found with all that work we did taking the samples through to the navigating cabin?"

The captain looked irritated at this query. He was waiting to organize the times for leaving so he said to Jonathon:

"You tell them Mr. Albany. But be quick about it. We are leaving later on this morning."

Jonathon's heart was pumping at this double assignment of activity that the captain was asking of him. So he addressed the men:

"I'm sure you don't want details of proportions of diamond bearing silt to ocean sand quantities. I can give it to you if you are interested . . . ."

The men looked glum at this putting of them down in the group and put out at Jonathon's standing up for himself. He now had the upper hand. A murmur of disinterest ran around the group. So there had been some progress made in diamond discovery. Assessing the situation the Captain announced:

"Right. Possessions packed up in two hours, men. The motorboat will be here at twelve midday. Then it's the trip to the coast and onto the two `planes for Great Britain and South Africa as has been directed.

The men were disturbed in their routine and scurried down below deck. They all found the trip dicey and passed by the locals armed in camouflage suits looking awesome but not acting threateningly. A flight attendant looking very efficient after what they had been doing on board ship hustled them onto the separate `planes. Jonathon managed to find a window seat in the plane allocated to him and settled with his tog bag containing his clothing. With a roar the `plane was winging its way through the steamy African skies southwards.

Chapter 6

Jonathon was making an effort to keep his wits about him at this now obvious change in circumstances with what his job contract required. Quite honestly he felt a sense of relief at leaving Sierra Leone. It had been an uncomfortable six week spell. His mind fell into what he would write in a report to the company executives. Basically they would have to realize that it would be nigh on two or tree lifetimes' work both out at sea off the coast and inland diggings at the source of the alluvial deposits inland in the third world African state of Sierra Leone.

He glanced out of the window. Both in Brazzaville and Luanda that was in Congo and Angola, political tensions were running high when they required the crew to be frisked quite roughly. Jonathon reacted patiently and so did the shift crew. It was a slightly better situation in Angola where Jonathon felt that he needed some fresh air and walked town onto the runway. Armed men surrounded the `plane. The situation seemed tense militarily speaking but they were left alone.

Then back to the aircraft all checked in aboard and the `plane flew on to Cape Town. Here Jonathon had gleaned the information that the life situation would become somewhat more civilized that was according to what he knew about leading his life in his future on board another diamond dredger anchored off the Orange River mouth where serious deep sea mining was taking place. The `plane landed at the only airport. He dwelt on the fact that this too was a politically tense country. There were anti communist activities in progress and an ironfisted clampdown by authorities.

What was occurring though they had been told was that there were forces at work trying to change Government in South Africa that had a grim control to the benefit of one section of the population. It was apparent that he had arrived right at a time when all this was set to change with anti-Government imprisoned leaders about to be freed from prison. They had been told to expect a lot of instability when they arrived.

All that the crew had been warned about that was to be expected in Cape Town when they arrived suddenly became very real. Jonathon stepped down off the `plane to the ministrations of tense nazi-like officials from what he could size up in the attitude being taken. English was spoken to the new arrivals the language in the arrival situation being tense and gutteral.

Jonathon felt that the atmosphere could be cut through like a knife action. He felt immediately that this was quite unpleasant. He and the men were obviously necessary in the circumstances but clearly not welcome at all. Grimfaced the leader of the officials spoke with a strong accent. Jonathon tried to place this way English was being used towards he and the crew. One of the officials said:

"Have you got transport into the city? A place to stay?"

Then Jonathon realized and linked up what they had been told by the company bosses. These officials were what was known as Afrikaners. Jonathon was not impressed by their curt and arrogant handling as he and the crew shift supplied their passports to enable them to leave for lodgings in the city. One of the officials continued speaking

"There is a bus to take you into Cape Town. You will have to go fast now to catch it before it leaves in half an hour's time."

Jonathon balked at this highhanded treatment from men who were obviously of his own western culture. They were all marched along the airstrip and into the vehicle. There followed a fairly scenic ride. The crew were dropped off at what was apparently a railway station entrance. Angrily their own leader quipped to Jonathon:

"Must we must fend for ourselves now?" Jonathon answered firmly:

"That is so. You have all got your accommodation directions as well as the date that the ocean going dredger leaves for the seas off the Orange River mouth north of where we are in Cape Town" Later the crew that were familiar faces now disappeared into the station complex. Jonathon pulled out of his pocket the letter the company had given to him in which his directions to his lodgings were included. He addressed the driver clearly a local man who seemed to know that Jonathon was to go to a boarding house above the town on the slopes of Table Mountain.

Stopping and starting at intersections through the city the vehicle halted finally outside a residence that Jonathon was dropped outside. He thought to himself this is not at all like home. It was high summer in the city on the slopes of Table Mountain and the sun baked down. He felt hot and flushed and desperately in need of a drink of cold water. Controlling his thirst and general discomfort he knocked on the entrance door that was in the shadows around at the side where there was an unkempt looking garden.

The door lock squeaked with disuse but was opened. Jonathon wiped his brow. A cool looking and attractive young blonde girl stood in the portal. In what Jonathon immediately worked out this was the Dutch Marijke that his mother had encouraged him to meet up with. Her presence made the situation a bit easier. She was bound to know if he could immediately get his thirst quencher. She spoke words that said what he already knew:

"Greetings. Yes. I am Marijke. You must be Jonathon who is going to work on contract on the diamond mining company ship."

Jonathon felt that this was the opportunity to get some cool, if not iced water. He was finding the discomfort of the Mediterranean heat driving him to impropriety. He said hoarsely:

"Can you find me some water to drink? I have just flown down West Africa with my shift crew and desperately need something to slake my thirst." The girl said:

"Of course. Welcome to Cape Town."

Jonathon wondered if she realized how thirsty he actually was. She said:

"Wait here." They had walked into a small living room that had the curtains drawn in the heat wave." Marijke said: "It is always hottest in the Cape in this area and at this time of the year. I am staying in a hotel nearby at my parents' expense. I will go and find you an iced drink."

Jonathon sunk down into an old but comfortable sofa. Then Marijke returned with a jug of water and a glass. She poured the sparkling and tempting water into the container carefully. At her handing it to him Jonathon could not wait to counter pleasantries with her. The water in the glass was even too cold to swallow down all at once so hot and bothered was he. After a while he felt human enough to converse with the girl. She clearly did not understand his discomfort and in their chatting mentioned:

"I have two friends in town that I have come to know in my working situation. They speak Afrikaans and their families' antecedents have lived in this part of South Africa, the Western Cape for centuries. I would like you to meet them. Perhaps we can see if they aware if there is a party somewhere that they know of tonight?"

The afternoon heat reached it's peak and Jonathon in the comfort of the old but comfortable sofa in the lounge began to feel better after he had swigged down another couple of the glasses of water in the dry heat. Marijke said:

"I don't like it here either but my parents have sent me to study at this University. My father works on the goldfields in the Transvaal but we are Dutch and he prefers me to be in Cape Town where there is more of a cultured learning atmosphere."

She spoke with a heavy accent that Jonathon realized was a Netherlands way of speaking English. For all his being a typically uncommunicative young male he threw in some monosyllables of response to her rather charming and halting dialect. He did not want to encourage any familiarity. This attitude of his was directly against his mother's wishes he was well aware when she started talking again:

"I suppose you are surprised to find me here waiting for you but my mother who works for the Dutch Embassy in Johannesburg told me that she had met up with your parents. They all seemed very keen that you and I meet up."

Jonathon was quiet trying to run his life. Yes this girl Marijke was attractive but she was not the familiar Jean of his knowing. Marijke continued talking typically feminine and clearly attracted to the exciting male adventure of what he had come to Cape Town for.

"How romantic to be working for a diamond mining company. My father told me that you have come straight down Africa from the diamond diggings in Sierra Leone. What was it like there?" Jonathon decided to cut the romantic illusions of this girl short. He answered:

"It probably sounds very exciting but it is no place for women. The country is constantly on the brink of civil war with children being used in the military situation."

Marijke was clearly put out at this information. Jonathon continued to disillusion her.

"Yes and there is thick jungle with the white beaches and palm trees studding the coastline but the tropical heat is intensive. Even here it is cooler." At these words she offered more water and said conversationally:

"I am sorry there is no ice cold beer for later on but the old lady who runs this pension is very strict and says she will not have alcohol on the premises." Jonathon replied:

"It does not matter. I was a serious student in Great Britain and did not spend much time taking drink although I enjoy a glass of beer from time to time." Then he changed the subject.

"What do you study? I seem to have arrived in yet another student situation." Marijke was vague in her answer:

"Oh just general arts. I am more interested in my two Afrikaans friends. I do not find the men here attractive in comparison to my Dutch compatriots. I have arranged to have them come over to meet you tomorrow evening."

Jonathon felt that he could at least show her some gratitude for finding him some friends of his own age, so thanked her. Then he asked

"Have they got male friends at all?" He changed the subject not waiting for a reply:

"I have been doing geological studies for the last three years in Scotland so never had an opportunity to socialize in London. There many expatriot South Africans are gathering to live, mostly English speaking I was told by some of my student friends."

Marijke broke in:

"Yes I can understand that because of the total clampdown the Government here has to make. And why? It is the communist threat to the country. I can speak more easily than my two Afrikaans friends because I grew up in the Netherlands and only recently with my parents in Africa. You will meet Marelize and Petronella whom I have told you about. Be very careful what you say to them about anything political. You may not know it but there are spies everywhere especially at this very liberal University we three girls are attending."

Jonathon looked a little put out and perturbed at what Marijke had just told him. It was clearly going to be difficult for an outsider to exist in what he could sense was an extremely tense political atmosphere. He responded:

"It's good that you told me of the situation people who are living here in. It is obvious that I will have to take great care in what I speak to the local girls who are your friends. How do they feel about all this?" Marijke looked slightly worried but then said:

"It is awkward for them and those of the same historical background because many of them have family stories interrelating to the peoples of other cultures that we from the outside world do not recognize democratically. The tide of events in South Africa over the last three hundred years or so has made them connected also to the very conservative rulers of the country. That is those who are holding out against communism and other matters that they see as a weakness in the governing of the country.

Many of the people whose forebears were the slaves in the distant past caused by interrelationships with local peoples have been practically tortured here, hence the sensation of tenseness in the country."

Jonathan looked very innocent Marijke thought. She said:

"You have a lot to learn here about the way people are being treated here. And it is ones like Marelize and

Petronella whose families are connected with the harsh treatment being dealt out to sections of the society in this land who are suffering." She went on for a few minutes more:

"Although I come from the same European country as Marelize and Petronella their families reach back for centuries here in South Africa. I have been doing some questioning and observing of the way the country is being forced socially, especially in what they call the Western Cape here. I have tried to find out what lies behind what seems to be hidden stories of their forbears, that was Dutch settlers coming to South Africa first in the seventeenth century, then Germans, and later the Huguenot French at the time of the persecution of the Catholic church, a time of religious upheaval in Europe. It was at these times and before in the seventeen hundreds that the slavery system came into existence."

She paused here because her words to Jonathon must have seemed very strange. He then said:

"So I will be meeting these two girls later today? This evening I think that you said?" Marijke answered:

"Yes. They are keen to meet someone like yourself who for a start is English and not just from English settler stock of the nineteenth century here but someone closely in touch with the Great Britain of the present. This I understand from my parents who as you know, your mother must have explained to you, that my mother is employed by the Netherlands Embassy in the Transvaal. You are a person who interests them."

Jonathon reacted to this by questioning her:

"Do they not take an interest in the English settler stock of people who came here originally then either?" Marijke said:

"Perhaps you don't know but there was within the last century a war here between the first European Settlers and the later English arrivals in South Africa. The tension and ill feeling is ongoing and the forced involvement in the Second World War of the South Africans has only made it worse especially with the present world wide Communist threat to the indigenous peoples."

Jonathon wanting to pave a smooth social path for himself in the visit that evening of the two Afrikaans girls as he had been prepared, listened as Marijke said:

"I would be curious to hear about their attitudes towards this tenseness in the Government clampdown in this country. Everything I am sensing here seems totally on edge." Marijke answered:

"They will not mind, no, because I know that they are two of many Afrikaners who do not support the more conservative regime that has an iron grip politically on this country. Such people as these two friends of mine have the difficult role of being connected also directly way back in time to the present, to the unpleasant situation of the Government holding sway here at this time."

Stifled laughter and controlled humor met Jonathon's ears at a knock at the front door of the boarding house. He sensed a feeling of arrogance as the footsteps of the two expected girls were heard tripping down the passageway down to the lounge, with curtains pulled to keep out the heat that was beating down in the late afternoon on the slopes of Table Mountain.

Two healthy looking attractive young women peered around the door at first curiously at the novel situation their student acquaintance Marijke had told them to expect. One was blonde haired and the other dark. The atmosphere of arrogance persisted and one of them, as Marijke a little later introduced them, said with what Jonathon picked up as forced impertinence:

"So! You are the Englishman that Marijke told us about. We are both my friend and I very pleased and interested to meet you. It is not often that people like us get to meet someone like you!"

Jonathon felt chuffed at this compliment but was a little uncertain, even a little put off by the high-handedness of their manner. As a perceptive young man he understood that these two girls were a section of the type of people clamping down in the Government. So he thought that he should as an alien in the situation say something tactful so responded to this somewhat arrogant address to him:

"Yes I am British and am trained to work on the diamond dredging barge off the Orange River estuary. My first assignment is starting this Saturday when I will report to a local airfield to be flown out by helicopter to the ship stationed off the South West African coastline."

The girls were pulled down a peg or two by this answer. Jonathon summed them up as tough young women. He was fascinated though as Marijke had told him that their families had existed for centuries in South Africa. This was an exciting experience to him. The two girls exchanged words incomprehensible to Jonathon, in Afrikaans. Marijke translated:

"They think you are what they call a "knap kêrel." That is someone who is clever and brave. They are fully aware of the dangers of this expedition you are undertaking."

More words were exchanged in the local language. Marijke explained again:

"Are you prepared to meet and work with the tough local people of the mixed origins of this country on board ship?" Jonathon was too confused to answer.

He was in a daze at being in this new country. He thought to himself again as they exchanged quick conversation in their language. He had visited Holland so realized a lot of the meaning of what was being spoke about. He picked up one phrase that was continually being repeated:

"Maar hy weet nie." That means, he thought grimly to himself: but he does not know. What did he not know?

In their presence Marijke looked picture of guilt as a go-between. She was basically of the same ancestry as that of the two Afrikaans girls, that was Dutch and French but over the last three centuries their families had lived thousands of miles apart in Europe and South Africa. He struggled to understand the gist of what they were saying. Then the penny dropped. It was obvious that they could clearly see that he knew very little about this country and the people who lived there. Then they addressed Marijke in Jonathon's hearing in halting English:

"We are very worried about the country that we live in. We are under pressure by outside forces." Petronella whispered anxiously: "The communist threat. It is so bad that we are forced to seek relief."

Jonathon did not quite understand her words until a party that had been talked about took place that evening with all that he was involving himself in. Petronella continued:

"We are such people who are in between the narrow minded government authorities and on the other side the peoples of mixed marriage who inhabit this part of the country in the south. We are being oppressed by the ruling party. Although we are of Dutch and Huguenot descent ourselves basically everyone here is interrelated.

The truth about the intermarriages that has been going on here for centuries is being repressed and the history of family stories by hearsay is being kept quiet. These facts are only spoken about amongst those connected with the governing sector of the land. We and others like us hate it but the Government has an iron fisted grip on this country."

Marijke broke in to this horrifying statement:

"It is only because you and I, Jonathon have lived on the outside of South Africa that we can talk like this. These two girls—he indicated Marelize and Petronella—are South African citizens unlike us, but I can tell you that there are anti government forces at work against the rulers of the system, both inside and beyond this land and its borders. There is a struggle on the go to overthrow the current oppressive regime."

Jonathon suddenly felt afraid at his role in the girls' presence. He was looking more and more perturbed as the girl spoke. What they were saying was putting forth a country completely unlike the one he had grown up in, Great Britain. The conversation was becoming stressful. He could understand that was the reason Marijke had invited them to meet the two Afrikaans girls. True to her mother who worked in the Dutch Embassy she said: "Petronella it's not all bad. Things are coming to ahead now in the anti-government struggle. It's not going to be many more months even now before they release the anti-authority leader."

Jonathon now felt he could speak to them in the discussion:

"Yes. There has been constant publicity of dislike and criticism of the current government in South Africa where I come from that is England."

Marijke said assertively:

"I know of a party that is happening tonight at one of the houses on the beachfront overlooking the sea on the other side of the mountain. I have my car so we can leave a little later when it's cooler to join the crown there." Petronella said: "I have brought some snacks." Jonathon looked hopeful at this because the last time he had eaten was some makeshift food on the helicopter that he had not enjoyed. He said:

"Will there be anything else to eat where we are headed for?" Marelize said: "I know some of the girls who will be there. Everybody has to eat so I know we will not go hungry."

Marijke drove carefully over the gap in the mountain to the party venue, with the other three in the car. On arrival there was a subdued hush at the newcomers. Marijke broke the ice saying: "Don't worry folks. I have brought an English guy with us to join the party. He is fresh out of England so has no anti-government or even government connections. You can all speak freely with him around."

The girls as he was to find a typically South African habit made straight for the group of other girls busy in the kitchen. At a loose end now missing Jean in the social situation like this he wandered over to a group of what he could only think of as rather untidily dressed male students, not at all like the acquaintances he had known in Scotland. One of them addressed him arrogantly:

"So what do you think of South Africa?" Immediately Jonathon rose to the bait as an outsider to the group:

"Something is going to happen very soon to end this grip your government has on this country. There are stories that I have heard in the newspapers that the indigenous peoples are even putting rocks and stones on the roads to curb the dominance by the conservative government that is holding sway here. Why is it like this? Can you give me a reason for this?"

He was keeping his end up in the argument amongst the men students. He did feel like a fish out of water though. Jonathon was becoming curious about the lives of these local people. They were so similar in type to himself but for centuries had lived many thousand miles apart in their ancestry. He asked outrightly:

"What have you got in common with what is well known outside this land to the apparently oppressed remnant of the slave population that has grown since the seventeenth centuries?"

His question was fobbed off. There were repressed sniggers at his enquiry and the conversation turned to the necessity of food and liquid nourishment for the time being.

Jonathon was determined to get to the root of his questioning as an outsider to these peoples in his presence. It seemed that they did have some connection to the indigenous peoples. Also from what he had heard there was included in the population living here, were peoples of Malay, Indians and Chinese descent.

Marijike realized that they would all have to have something to eat and drink so she interrupted and ushered the group to the eating area. The pressure was easing in Jonathon's questioning as to the root of the stressful political situation in the country that was to be the circumstances for his work on board the diamond mining dredger vessel out at sea up the coast. There was now the thought of something to eat and drink. He remembered that he had arranged his entrance and exit keys to the boarding house where there was sleeping accommodation. He had looked in at the landlady's office and had told her that he would be back later in the evening. All he had got from her was a hardly audible sullen assent. He wondered if she was of the same local descent as the Afrikaans girls. She was many years older that he could see.

When the group of young people in Jonathon's party had arrived at the beachfront they found the party in full swing. There was though a hushed conversation ensuing amongst the Afrikaans partygoers. It soon became clear to Jonathon that they and their friends were only too pleased to have an outsider like himself to give some input into the situation that they with their Huguenot and Dutch forbears had lived with for centuries. Untidily dressed young people, the men some of them with long hair as was fashionable, together with women partners and other hangers seemed to be coming and going in and out of the wooden cottage on the slope of the mountain leading down to the beach.

The sea was sparkling into the near distance with the electric lighting from the cottages in the surrounds. Loud drumming and a whining sound of steel guitars met their ears. The music was loud. Jonathon perceived that this was especially intended to drown out any embarrassing lapse in conversation amongst the partygoers.

Jonathon stood pensively at the entrance to the darkened room. There seemed to be a medley of young people wearing tight pants and loose colored t-shirts and for the men scruffy shirts. No one looked very purposeful and steel guitars music was drowning out any conversation transpiring. Young people were coming and going past him through the entrance seemingly intent on their own lives.

There did however seem to be a hard core of party goers locked in conversation Because he did not want to lose his lift back to the boarding house and as he was due to join his ship the diamond barge dredger tomorrow by eleven, he stuck close to Marijke and her two Afrikaans friends. The group they joined mainly male students greeted Jonathon as he joined them. Petronella, also with them said forthrightly:

"And what are we talking about this evening? You know I told you that it was my family ancestors who held control in the early days of the greater part of the land in the Stellenbosch district. Our family have held the winelands in their hands by descent for hundreds of years."

One of the young men said:

"We know that. But who controlled the workers, the slaves? Without them the Boland could not be worked." Marelize joined in the cut and thrust of the conversation. In opposition:

"You know very well that it was my father's family who organized the workers on the farms that were gradually divided up amongst the sons and grandsons and even their forbears that were the early Huguenot settlers."

The conversation was mostly in Afrikaans and Jonathon was absorbing mentally with great interest all that was being said. It seemed the centuries old spite of competition amongst the early Huguenots was coming to the fore. Mustering up an assertiveness that he was not actually feeling very sure about amongst these people he did not know at all well he dared to join in. After all they were all young people with a future to live out.

"Yes. I have just arrived from the diamond fields in Sierra Leone and before that from Great Britain and I can tell you South Africa is not popular there because of the way some of its people are being treated." One of the Afrikaans students quipped:

"So what can we do to change the traditions that have continued her for centuries? How do you think the slave population began here?"

There were concerted sniggers all round the group. A supporter of Dirk's said forcibly:

"Yes. And what were the Dutch settlers to do to establish themselves in the new countries that they had reached by sailing out from Holland to make a livelihood in this country all those years ago?" Dirk backed his friend up. Jonathon was listening attentively:

"Yes the Dutch women when they were allowed to come out to the new land stayed pure of blood but the men had no option but to appease the local inhabitants by intermarriage, that was a kind of polygamy. Think about it. How do you think their Dutch women felt about that? I am sure that they would have liked to remain pure in both their religious belief and social behavior towards their men folk." At this point Marelize broke in:

"Yes our Huguenot antecedents stayed pure in their relationships with their partners. I know this from family hearsay that has been passed down from mother to child."

The atmosphere was growing tense. The men in the group grew restless and began to hope for some means to quieten the bickering that was beginning amongst the girls as to who the dominating people were in the olden days. That was when the farms were being divided when the old tillers of the land passed what they had worked on to their descendents. Petronella said:

"Yes it was my old ancestors who ran the Paarl valley and introduced the French tradition of vineyards into the area. Marelize was quick to quip with an answer, saying:

"My old folk were cleverer than that. They knew there were migrant wandering and feckless groups of people with both indigenous and European antecedents who could be used in the farming effort. Yes my people made them build little laborers cottages on this land, here in Stellenbosch and Paarl and also inland as the years passed on. It was an exciting new project with all involved, with a purpose for the future. The climate was ideal for the vine growing.

It was clear that there was a vast area of God's land as my people called it where the migrant slaves could be used to help farm their land as my people called it. The Huguenot settlers coming from France in the eighteenth century instilled in these slaves the age old French tradition of wine viticulture. The tradition is with us today. As from old it was a money earner, a livelihood for all."

The conversation was becoming argumentative and heavy and the men in the party were clearly not approving of the women's boasting and taking control of the social situation. Of course the men, typical of their sex had little to say. Dirk, who was one of the men pulled of his pocket a carton of cigarettes and offered them around hoping to quell the tenseness. This of course made it worse and another of the men pulled out a rough looking holder containing what also looked like carelessly formed smoking objects.

The thought flashed through Jonathon's mind that in the struggle against the grip the government that the people were living with this was forcing them to seek relief. But what was this relief? Was the present offering of what in all appearances seemed to be some sort of smoking part of this struggle? Being a male and young Jonathon noticed this immediately but did not realize that the substance being proffered to him were in fact soft drugs. He had not come across this sort of smoking before as it was not permitted in Great Britain. He observed that the young person looked sloppy and sneaky in comparison to Dirk and the few slightly smarter looking young male students.

The person was taking advantage of Jonathon's curiosity about him. An outsider and new to the country, Jonathon thought to himself at least he looks more relaxed than the others in this core group although he did look a bit of a hanger on to the others.

Settling in a more relaxed manner in what was now rapidly becoming a smoke haze Jonathon tried to communicate with the others in the group. The sloppy looking young pushed his box of smoking offerings towards Jonathon saying with eyes sparking and sneakily flashing all round him, obviously hoping not to be noticed in what he was doing in the increasing smoke pall permeating the party He said in what Jonathon was quite aware was an underhand tone: "Have one." In all appearances it was a generous gesture but Jonathon had no idea what he was letting himself in for

Jonathon was an innocent in this group of South Africans that Marijke had led him into in the party that they had come to. When she saw that smoking was underway she immediately in the clean Dutch tradition that was her nationality said forthrightly:

"No smoking allowed here." No one of course took any notice of her standpoint. Here again Jonathon felt his mother's influence on the situation that he found himself forced into. He felt obliged to stand up for his manhood amongst these young men of his own age, to accept what was being offered.

He thought unknowing of the hold such smoking could have on someone for life, even incapacitating daily routine activities, that he should accept what was being offered. The men in the group, although he did wonder if he was imagining it, were looking sneaky and behaving in what seemed to him in a very underhand manner. The aroma of what was being smoked hit his nostrils unpleasantly. Seeing that he was an outsider the more shabbily dressed and poorly behaved youngster took his chance and looked even more evilly satisfied when Jonathon under pressure now from the smoke pall in the group accepted the offer. He was at a loss to know what to do with it, but obviously it had to burn while hanging from his mouth. The one who had made the offer, as expected by Jonathon said:

"Here—I'll light up for you. I'm having one myself. Little did Jonathon know at the time, duped as he was becoming in the company of smokers, that he was a victim of a marijuana drug addict's temptation. Marijke also felt this behavior was quite innocent because Jonathon being the male of the species had taken the lead. She had found in her time in South Africa that a lot of people smoked. But she also did not realize that this was a marijuana drug smoking incident.

As the drug began to have its effect Jonathon began to stagger around amongst the group with the flashes in his brain lessening his tension while the conversation whipped around the core group concerning past envy of Huguenot masters because of covetousness of numbers of slaves and possession of tracts of land in the historical opening up of the new country.

Marijke was keeping her head because she had to drive Jonathon and her two Afrikaans friends back to their overnight lodgings. She saw that Jonathon was not behaving normally. She spoke urgently:

"Jonathon! Have you been drinking?"

Jonathon was hardly aware of what was transpiring in his now drugged state.

Chapter 7

He woke up the next morning feeling very much the worse for wear both mentally and physically. The suburban boarding house was quiet and impersonal. He could hear dishes being washed in what must be a kitchen further off. That didn't improve matters because he realized that he must have missed breakfast at the residence. Wryly his thoughts dwelt on the fact that in his state of unease and continuing dizziness from the party and all it had involved him in the night before he did not even feel hunger pangs.

With a shock he realized that he was due at the airport once again to fly up to the alluvial mining operations that were some way up the coast to the north west of the country. Why he had even had to come to Cape Town he failed to see but on thinking about it supposed that in this more permanent base of his part in the mining contract he had to know where his home from home was that was here.

The dizziness did not pass as he fumbled in washing, shaving and dressing as aptly as he thought suitable for a day aboard ship. Suddenly he realized with a shock that there was no sign of Marijke or her two Afrikaans girlfriends. He must have made a right fool of himself both at the student party and at his return back to the boarding house. His head was still swimming. He recalled the heavy smoke haze at the party.

Was this what involvement in the nicotine habit did to a person? He recalled the heavy smoke haze at the party. He did not realize that it was an addictive soft drug that had been sneakily given to him, passing it off as just a cigarette. He staggered around not comprehending why he had this dazed feeling in his head of not being able to focus. He managed to stuff his clothes that he had used the night before into his tog bag and located the landlady to acquire a key to the premises. She was just finishing the beginning of her household chores.

Quite used to the scruffiness of the floating population of young people in and out of her boarding house she inquired:

"You arrived last evening didn't you?" "Yes," replied Jonathon dimly at her rather pointed attitude. "I will need to have a key to the house."

The woman went off to a side room and fetched it and gave it to him. Jonathon said:

"I have to be off now. I'll be gone for a six week stint up the coast doing diamond mining off a ship."

The old woman looked curious and impressed. She could see that he was not a young person of the usual sort she had come across by her dealings with the floating student population in her boarding house.

After what had happened in the claustrophobic haze of whatever had been smoked last night, he did not know what it was, and his uncontrolled staggering around the moving partygoers last night, Jonathon felt quite nauseous. Then events of the night before vanished from his mind as he stepped out into the cool clear morning outside. His head was still swimming though and he groped his way by bus and train out to the air station. once again.

He had to walk quite far but eventually found a group of men near a small aircraft, a helicopter. A couple of fairly smartly dressed individuals were obviously to Jonathon going to pilot them all up north to the Namibian desert coast surrounding the estuary of the Orange River. Jonathon had been told by the company that he was expected at the airfield by one o' clock that day. A little desperately he looked at his watch. Yes, there was still time. He thought he had time enough to make his presence known to the group of locals who were now there and staring curiously, but also talking in a coarse though reliably matter of fact manner amongst themselves. It flashed through his mind that these were the sort of people that he could now dimly remember from last night that had been referred to as the antecedents of the slave population in South Africa. He remembered that he had been warned that there was a near explosive situation in the country regarding such people so a little nervously he approached them. They greeted him with unexpected humility.

Obviously they were the replacement of the English manual workers in the company who had been sent back to the United Kingdom from West Africa. To his dazed nod of greeting in a humble though rough manner they spoke as one:

"Môre baas. You lead us this time? The other baas he could not come today. It was too much hard work for him. But us people we need someone to tell us what to do. Jus, we know what is the work but Baas, you must tell us if we do it right. That new Baas Meneer is you."

Jonathon felt very strange in coming to this new country and suddenly without his own fellow British countrymen, having to be part of all this. He thought he had better make some communicative gesture of speech so said:

"Yes. Thank you for welcoming me. I am a little bit worried to go onto this ship. But you will all help me I know."

He had tried to simplify the language he was using as they clearly had their own manner of speech. They said together:

"Jus. We get on the aeroplane now Meneer. We jus go to the man who takes the aeroplane up in the sky for us, to the ship. He is going soon. If he mus make us wait then jus, we mus all wait for him, the pilot Baas."

Jonathon found himself on the bare and desolate airfield that was now a long way out of town and far from the comfortable boardinghouse that he would not see again for six weeks. He summed up the situation. It was clear from the pilots' brisk actions that he and the group were now required to board the helicopter. They all one by one hoisted themselves aboard. It was a slightly better feeling to Jonathon to be sheltered in the aircraft.

The wind was blowing dust everywhere and the day was heating up uncomfortably. The men who were he and the crew were squashed together irritably as the chopper after a crashingly roaring sound with its heavy load of people, took off vertically for some way upwards. Then it took a direction for what Jonathon presumed was northwards.

Jonathon had a quick word of introduction in his position with the team with the pilots and had been told that they were en route to a landing strip just north of the Orange River mouth where they would land in the early afternoon. After that the two pilots had said they would head to wherever the diamond mining barge was lying off the coast. This would take an hour or so.

Jonathon heard vaguely an offer of food being made to him. He was nervous of this flight so was not feeling very hungry. He realized though that he would have to keep his body functions going. He supposed that he should have prepared something to eat for the trip but thankfully here was an offer of food being provided for him. One of the crew spoke as they flew. Jonathon could hardly hear him over the `plane's engine motors.

"Baas, you must eat something. Here is a toebroodjie, you can have it if you want."

Jonathon could just hear the man's words. He was deeply impressed by the kindness of the person. With a nervous gulp he accepted the offer saying:

"Thank you brother. I did not bring anything for myself you are right. It seems that I will have nothing otherwise until we reach the ship." The spokesman for the group said:

"We will have something for a supper by tonight. Us people have been on this route before three times so know that we mus bring the sandwiches with us."

Jonathon's dazed thinking came together a little as he digested the sandwich proffered him. Half alert only in his thinking he looked out of the helicopter. Below the earth was gradually turning into white sandy desert. They must be nearing Namibia where they would land then take off again for the ship the "Agulhas" their working contract barge.

Even though the proferred sandwich that he had eaten slowly while looking down on the earth below was making him feel slightly nauseous he was grateful for something to fill him.

The helicopter motor was making them all shake but it seemed that the journey by air was almost over. Jonathon could sense a slight relaxation amongst the group of men that he was with. They murmured and muttered amongst themselves half audibly above the roar of the engine. Jonathon tried to hear what they were saying. He caught the words of the man nearest to him

"We go down now. Hou vas."

The chopper jerked as the pilot changed the direction. Jonathon felt his stomach turn as they went ricketting downwards. The rotors above the aircraft beat regularly. Jonathon did not want to look downwards. With a shudder then the helicopter's wheels met the sand where there was a desolate open space for the pilots to land. One of the crew members bravely joked:

"Almal out nou!"

Jonathon's face was turned away from the helicopter for some fresh air while the pilots took direction. The same man seeing Jonathon's reaction of fear said:

"Kom nou baas."

Jonathon felt a little eased as the engine of the helicopter suddenly fell silent. Like a schoolboy he joined the surge to get out into the fresh air. The wind outside was whipping the sand around and they were all soon covered in what was blowing outside. Jonathon caught a shallow breath. The crew stood round in a circle trying to avoid the particles of sand blowing into their eyes ears and mouth. There was nothing for it but to join them and that he did. Then after what seemed a long while the door of the pilots' cabin sung open and one of the two pilots ordered:

"Back on board men. We want to take off for the "Agulhas" out there at sea."

Jonathon who was still suffering the after effects of the digestion of the rather stale sandwich trooped on board with the rest. It did not seem that he was going to be in control as his employer's contract had stated. These men he was with were obviously very tough people

They were all glad to be out of the wind though were now facing the bumpy ride over the sea to the diamond mining barge out at sea. Jonathon had tried to focus on the ship while waiting to take off again. It was, in what he had glimpsed an ominous dark shape quite some way out in the ocean away from the land. He had an awful feeling that what was to happen there was not going to be pleasant or easy. He already had the feeling that the small quota of rough though efficient seeming locals had no illusion about his capability to take charge.

He felt uneasy about this. The captain on the ship up north in Sierra Leone had been not too difficult to deal with at least he had been English speaking. But from what he had observed of the almost Nazi like handling of his initial reception in South Africa he had forebodings about what to expect when they finally landed on the "Agulhas."

He thought to himself: had Tasha his mother been right in saying that he was taking on more than he could handle, that it was too difficult and dangerous? He looked out of the chopper and could see the huge coastal estuary of the Orange River down below. Then all that he could sight was the ocean swells below as they neared the "Agulhas." Then the chopper hovered over the ship. Jonathon caught a tight breath. One of the shift crew said:

"Nou us go down."

The chopper was descending. Dark figures of men seemed to be darting around aboard what seemed to be the stern of the ship. Crackle from the voice over the electronic system in the pilots' cabin came to the mens' ears, but it was too noisy to hear what was being said. Then Jonathon could pick up the conversation from the pilot's side. Yes. That was what the pilot in control was saying:

"Deck cleared. We are ready to land."

Jonathon swallowed in fear but was sure that they were going to land safely. His head began to swim again in the tension of the day's activities and what now seemed dazedly obvious to him. It was obvious that he was now feeling the after effects of the smoke and some sort of drug in the smoking that had been offered to him the night before. Jonathon felt afraid. Then with a bang and a shudder the helicopter hit the deck of the "Agulhas." Shouting ensued from the waiting men on deck.

For all their tough looking outward appearance the shift crew that the helicopter had ferried him with out to sea, were clearly relieved. Comments fell harshly onto Jonathon's ears from the men with him. He heard:

"We is here now. On the ship almal. We spring uit op die skeep. Almal ready nou. Die chopper is down."

This was not unlike what Jonathon was experiencing in his feelings about this terrifyingly exciting trip. At least that is what it was seeming like to him. What sense of reality he had matured with as a student knocked at his thinking at these moments as the men grabbed their few possessions and began to jump onto the stern deck of the diamond mining barge the "Agulhas." He suddenly thought in a near panic state: am I fit enough even to jump out like these men? He had left it that it was he who was last out.

One of the pilots opened the door to the head of the chopper and was unfastening his ear muffling apparatus worn to protect his hearing. Sharply he said to his co-pilot:

"Are you ready Brent? Is every thing switched off?"

Intrigued by this situation, but preparing to land with his few possessions he heard one of the two pilots say:

"Are you going down first? You had better jump off now. The men have left you space to land. We are in a hurry now as we need to make a report to the Captain of the ship for a confirmation of the trip to the company."

Jonathon strung his thoughts together He said at a loss for words:

"Yes sir. A record of the trip."

The two men were, he could see, slightly older than himself. He thought that he had better make his descent onto the deck immediately. He looked down and then jumped off. It was not too far to go to land on board the deck. With a controlled shout to him to clear the landing space that he did by moving away from where the two pilots needed to be he found himself in the company of a few of what he had come to expect since reaching this country for the first time, what seemed like militarily operational and harsh sounding men.

They spoke also in the local language that he had heard the night before. It was late afternoon by now. He clung to his possessions, what few he had with him. One of the men clearly the Captain in an untidy looking uniform, addressed him:

"So meneer! Jy is hier. Dank die here!"

Jonathon thought that he had better respond in what seemed to him to be an overbearing attitude that was being taken towards him.

The captain and what seemed to be two officers who were clearly the head person's two henchman looked Jonathon up and down. It was obvious that they had not come across someone like him before or if they had, very seldom. Covert glances and unfriendly suppressed smiles played around the three men's lips. Suddenly Jonathon felt very alone in this predicament. It was clear that Tasha had been quite right in her opposition to what he was now quite clearly involved in.

Suddenly everything seemed very real. The ship was swaying to and fro and up and down. He glanced back at the chopper. No chance of getting out of this situation that way. The two pilots were communicating to one another. A distant drone of what must be the engine of the diamond dredger could be heard. Seagulls swooped overhead mewing. What was he expected to say to these men? He did not like the look of them and they in their turn clearly were not going to waste any sympathy on him. He had seen that the ship's crew that he had arrived with had already disappeared down below. They would have been friendlier towards him he was sure, than these three men who looked like real ogres.

The smoke pall from the night's partying the evening before again made his head swim, so he said nothing. One of the two officers was a little more sympathic looking than the other two and he spoke above the splashing of the ocean that lapped against the sides of the "Agulhas."

""So Meneer. You know what to do. The baas of the company has told us that you were coming on the chopper.

Jonathon recognized the type of dialogue that the man was using from the student group at the party the night before. How could he tell these men that he needed to lie down? That the sudden impetus from being in the air in the chopper, to the swaying boat was making feel nauseous. This and Tasha's highly strung nervousness and warnings came to him to take care in what he was doing. Suddenly he wished that he had taken her advice and had gone for a landlubber job.

This situation though had seemed so enticing so exciting at first. Surely these men knew the commonest language in the world. He broke into speech:

"May I talk in English please?"

The men's eyes went from him arrogantly to one another. In broken English once again they replied.

It was clear to Jonathon that these three men were not only complete strangers to him but that they were out to what in English terms, was to rib him. They knew that they were the dominant masters in the situation aboard not only holding their arrogance in force over him but also most definitely over the locals who had been kind enough to share their sandwiches with him. These crew members would be doing most of the donkey work such as Jonathon had experienced of dredging up the ocean bed's silt that had been washed down river from the alluvial diamond bearing area much further inland that was at this time Kimberley up the river some many kilometers away upstream.

By now Jonathon was on his last legs and just needed to flop down on a cabin bunk and turn over on his side and fall into a deep slumber. But this last thought was interrupted with harsh words penetrating his brain in the already completely confused state that he was in.

"So Meneer! Nou gaan ons werk."

Dimly Jonathon felt totally defeated. The Captain was expecting him to function in a work situation at this time of day. And after what he had experienced during the rest of the time since he had awoken in a crazed stupor at the boarding house on the slopes of Table Mountain in Cape Town. Perhaps the man in charge of the dredger ship where he found himself at this moment was testing him. Oh! That must be it!

Time, yes moved far more slowly in this land than in Great Britain. Of course. The man began to mix his Afrikaans tongue with the English language. He spoke gutturally:

"You sleep tonight. I'll take you below deck to the cabin for you and one of the crew will see you into the eating area in an hour or so. First unpack."

Then he spoke in Afrikaans to one of the two Officers.

"Die Engelsman. Hy het sy eie slaapplek."

At these words Jonathon was very relieved, for it was obvious in his present state he would not only have to arrange his belongings, the few that he had brought with him and make a final effort in the day ahead to pull himself together in a working situation for tomorrow. After the Captain had spoken one of the officers ushered him forcefully into the lower parts of the ship and down a badly maintained passageway into an unfriendly looking cabin. The man said:

"There is your sleeping place. I will come back in one hour to take you to the eating room."

Jonathon was by now so tired and confused by the action of the day even though he was young, that he just flopped down on the rough seeming cabin bunk. His aching muscles relaxed slightly. He thought: now just give me fifteen minutes to clear my mind. He suddenly felt drowsy. No, he could not sleep yet. It was too early in the evening. The officer had said he would be back. His head was swimming still. At least he felt sleepy enough to know that he would be able to get a good night's rest.

At this idea he felt a little better but quaked in his whole body's frame at the thinking of apparently having to face the rough looking crew at the coming meal. They were a completely different set of people to the type of those that he had known back home in Great Britain.

Thinking this over as he lay there in what was left of his brain's functioning he decided that these people he had come with to the dredger the "Agulhas" seemed somehow to be warmer of heart than the rather meanly teasing class of manual workers that he had experience with in West Africa. But they had looked very tough and were obviously not going to tolerate any weakness of behavior, even direct taking of the upper hand with any of their group. This even though he was designated to be their superior as he and the captain and officers did know.

Suddenly the next day dawned. In Jonathon waking experience there was a loud thumping on the door of the cabin where he had lain down to sleep the night before. The swaying of the ship and the emptiness of his stomach made him realize that he was still feeling nauseous. This was seasickness. He tried to pull himself together in the early light.

He could hear the ocean outside. Huge swells gushed at the side of the dredger barge. He stumbled off the cabin bed and felt blindly for his clothes in his large tog bag as he wondered where the washing facilities were. He had not brought too much with him. No time for guessing where the ship's laundry was.

Jogging his senses now the door was flung open and the rather scruffy looking officer appeared and said:

"Ja, you was lying down I can see. There is no time for that here. There is work to be done today. Kom nou. The food is ready. I show you where." The man left.

It was now obvious to Jonathon that he was he going to be cruelly used aboard this ship between the nazi like officers and subservient crew. Also in the present feeling of the stress that the smoking had left him with from the party two night ago, he was going to end up being the scapegoat in the situation.

There was more thudding on the door. Someone was shouting at him from outside. Having dressed he though that he had better see what the person outside wanted. He opened the door of his quarters. A rough looking crew hand was fumbling with the door with the words:

"The breakfast is ready sir. The captain he say you must come to the dining cabin very soon. Is you ready sir?"

His stomach tight with hunger and still feeling the effects of the party two nights ago, Jonathon tried to adjust to the new day. He summoned up an answer to the man:

"Yes! Yes I'm coming. Just direct me to the breakfast eating cabin. I'm still very new here."

The man stopped in his tracks and said a little sympathically, Jonathon thought for all the rough handling that he was having:

"Are you alright sir? You look a bit sick. It's the sea outside that makes it like that. You can ask at the desk on the way to the dining cabin for some anti seasickness tablets. Yes. Its that way. I will go with you."

Jonathon had started walking unsteadily in the way the man had pointed to. He lurched along the gangway some way and shortly afterwards the two found a sleepy looking night duty officer packing up after his night's shift work. Jonathon approached him not keen though to show how queasy he was feeling. He managed to blurt out the words:

"This deck hand told me that I can get some sea seasickness medicines here. Is that right?"

The deck hand on duty at the end of his tether now that his shift was over for the night scrabbled around in an untidy looking cupboard finally finding the half full bottle of medicine. He handed it to Jonathon saying:

"The instructions for taking the tablets are on the bottle. It should do the trick in helping you adjust to the ocean swells."

Jonathon answered:

"Thank you man. Which way to the breakfast galley from here?"

The man waved his arm in the direction to the left in the maze of gangways leading off the main reception area. Jonathon heard surly early morning voices coming from behind a closed door at the end of the passage he was stumbling down as the ship swayed quite heavily to and fro. Even though the crew hand was with him he was most uncertain as to the reception he would receive upon entering the galley.

Maybe though it would not be that bad. Maybe he was just feeling hungry. With no evidence of tasteful behavior the crew hand with him burst into the eating quarters where the deck hands were gathered, with Jonathon in tow. The same group of rough deck hands were well into the breakfast stage in the morning's proceedings. They seemed locked in conversation but all looked up when he entered the galley. The most loquacious of the men, seemingly a leader of sorts spoke to Jonathon as he found a chair to sit down on.

"Morning baas. You will be the man to show us what to do with the dredging today. We must first make the drop basket ready with the heavy weights to make the drop to sink it into the sea. You know we work from the deck to scrape the samples from the sea sand at the bottom."

All this seemed very basic to Jonathon although from what he had experienced in like waters off Sierra Leone there was a good deal of mathematical sounding depths and location of the ship's position to be taken into account too. The meal finished and the men stumbed with their newly found sea legs, onto the deck.

The apparatus that they would be using was heaped neatly on a pile at one side of the deck. Gradually it became clear what they would have to do. Eventually Jonathon got the men to drop the plummet line into the ocean to test the depth of the sea where they were anchored. He also took bearings towards the river mouth and tested the salt water for the amount of fresh water being washed down from the Orange river estuary

Jonathon was somewhat less impressed now by the company he had to keep for the time of six weeks that he would be working as a supervisor on board the diamond dredging barge the "Agulhas." As he and the group of men moved noisily out of their chairs from the breakfast table Jonathon began the wonder where the captain and two officers were who had so peremptorily welcomed him onto the vessel from the helicopter on alighting the day before.

Of course shortly after climbing the ship's ladder onto the deck where they would all be working, the senior officers made their presence known at the start of the day's work. They looked a grim trio, the captain and his two henchmen but at least when the captain spoke Jonathon felt there was some sort of leadership ensuing for the day.

The chief person aboard addressed the men as they noisily one by one climber the ladder up to the open sea air above:

"Reg nou mense. Almal together in a group over to the side by the working apparatus, the drop basket and haulage. Jy!" He addressed a straggler who was having trouble with a shoe lace. "Gou nou. We must begin work. It is after nine this morning already. We are already late. Jy!" Again Jonathon was summarily called in these terms as the captain waved an arm at him. "Jou must take charge here now. You can see what these men must do!

We have an urgent radio message coming through in two hours that we have been given notice of by the company. Myself and the officers here will be back to see what you are doing before lunch. Ja nou. Get busy."

Jonathon was still feeling queasy and it was getting worse. He thought that it would be best to but on some sort of an act in the situation now because he did not feel any sort of superiority towards these men. He had also had very little experience with people like these.

They stooged around in a group and stared covertly at Jonathon. Of course they wanted some sort of leadership from him. Surely they knew what to do? Desperately Jonathon taking the bull by the horns said firmly mustering up courage and speaking into the sea breeze:

"Alright! Get started now!"

This seemed all that was needed in the working situation for the time being.

Chapter 8

An ominous feeling set into both Jonathon's already nervous state that he was in, and the uncertainty of his new duties. He also was experiencing this continual sense of what was being induced in him by his mother's attitude as to the danger of the work he was doing.

It was ongoing at present while supervising the men under him, but there was a nagging feeling in his brain of what was in another radio message coming through, apparently over the radio connection to the Head Office of the company.

The continual measuring and analyzing of the ocean bed's depths and the samples the men were bringing up was becoming boring and tiring. There was a sharp but cool wind blowing off the desert coast blustery with ozone and the salt filled air tingled on the men's bodies as they worked.

Then the dreaded message came to him via what the captain had picked up from the ship's radio communication. The stiff looking captain, clearly not intending to offer any sympathy, came up to Jonathon after striding across the deck towards him. He reached the place where the young British man and the deckhands were grouped at work. Nastily with obviously no overreaction of sentiment in the news that he had to impart, he announced to Jonathon, who had no privacy in the situation:

"I have seriously bad news for you my man." Jonathon quailed. Had he lost his job? Was that It? But no. The captain continued:

"It is clear through radio information just received that your mother has died. I have to tell you that she has committed suicide."

Jonathon quite naturally stunned at this news felt a faint feeling of paling in his face and an almost electric shock like sense of tremors running through his body. The captain for all the harshness of his tone, completely lacking in even any empathy in the information that he had just imparted, said:

"You had better go down to the kitchen galley area and ask the steward on duty there for a couple of thickly sugared cups of tea. Perhaps that will help you." Was Jonathon imagining it? Was the man softening in his attitude, if that was possible, with the almost unkind nature that he obviously had?

He staggered in both mind and body away from the group of men at work. During the time that he had been told the shocking news the men could clearly hear that something drastic had happened in Jonathon's life. This only served to make him feel worse. Now there would be underhand whisperings and assumptions as to what had gone wrong with their bossman.

Bitterly to add insult to injury he could still feel the after effects of the drug that he had been coerced into taking the night before the last one at the party. He felt absolutely sick with worry and shock, not to mention a sense of anger at himself for being involved in all this.

One of the deck hands was shouting at him trying to communicate with him in his shock. Was this some sort of human feeling being shown him, some sort of realization by someone else at what he was experiencing? In his state of near stupor the man took his arm and said:

"Kom baas. I'll guide you to the galley. I heard the captain say that you mus have a couple of strong cups of tea heavily sugared to pull you right for the moment. Heavily sweetened the Capatin said. Come now baas. Lets walk to the ship's ladder to the galley. I'll help you down. The sheer kindness of the man by comparison to the captain's harsh reaction towards him at his staggering news, touched him and gave his now near broken heart a little upliftment, even just a little. Hardly knowing what he was saying he said, not caring that he did not really know who was listening:

"It's my mother. She's dead. She died yesterday. She took her own life. Listening intently the man, when they had reached the kitchen galley, said:

"That must be the worst news a man can get. Eespecially in a working day like this that we are in. Here now the captain has been on his walkie talkie to this galley hand. There is a strong heavily sugared cup of tea waiting to keep you going, and a cheese sandwich also."

Jonathon could hardly take in the only sympathy possible to accept that was being shown to him. Finished the repast offered he lent forward on the chair, face pale and put his head in his hands. He was in despair. He had a now unexpectedly compassionate acquaintance. Depression hit him right in the center of his forehead while he sat there as the captain had given him the time to recoup his selfcontrol. The work hand assigned to him in this crisis knew about the shocking experience that Jonathon had that morning, from the message that the company's headquarters had sent through.

As the urgent minutes ticked by he slowly lifted his head and opened his eyes. Yes there was another human being sitting nearby. Not of his own nationality as he had found so many of the people in this country to be but nevertheless appearing from the expression on his tough work wizened face and the words being spoken to him, to have at least a jot of sympathy for the unfortunate young man:

"Dis jou ma who is dead. Ja, ek weet. I also lost my mother jus a few years back. She was everything a young man could want. She cooked like an angel. When there was trouble with my father or brothers and sisters—yes—we was a big famelie—she was always the one to put it all right. She pulled us all up. I will never know where she got her strength from She worked for us, cooked, yes and cleaned for us. I am still to this day missing her."

At these words Jonathon felt shaken to the core. Could he honestly say such things about Tasha? As the two men in the same predicament though as different as chalk from cheese, sat there their experiences in common did an iota of comforting of one another. Jonathon had to blurt out some communicative words at this man's response:

"My mother has taken her own life. I think it is my fault." The man immediately replied in a fatherly way:

"Jou mus not think like that. That is a bad thing to do, to make her death your fault. But I see, she was your mother."

The man hesitated struck with compassion at the young man's pathetic plight. A strong character as Jonathon was finding these local people to be, the man spoke again:

"It will be for the best to go back on deck and get on with the haulage. The workmen need you there up on deck. It will be no good for you to go to your cabin and suffer and think about this alone." Somehow Jonathon found strength in the logic of the man's encouraging words.

The man that he was conversing with, so conveniety there as another human being took the lead by putting into practice his words just spoken. Jonathon's eyes followed his movements. The local man, as Jonathon was coming to know these people, rose slowly and awkwardly from the chair.

Yes, Jonathon could see that as a man at least fifteen years his senior, his body was showing the taking of strain in the haulage up and down in and out of the ocean bed over the ship's rails, the letting down of the scraper drop basket that pulled the samples of ever hopefully diamond bearing, silt out of the sea. Jonathon tried to make an effort at the man's attempt at consolation.

Yes, he was tying up in his mind the situation that he found himself in this country that was so completely new to him. Somehow this other person was realizing that it was something of a crisis situation for this new young man. From the yokel's point of view Jonathon was not at all like the usual harsh and domineering type of men, the officers who always seemed to have the upper hand with he and his fellow workers on board.

Yes, not like the captain and officers at all. Those men never gave he and the deckhand even one chance in the mornings to take even a breath of air or to take it easy for just a minute or two. They were all worked like the slaves that he knew his people were descended from by family hearsay. But things were changing in the government now. He thought to himself: yes there's a lot of us who won't take a soft tongue from him who tell us how to do our work. Yes, like this young man was doing.

So did the captain and officers not have a point in their harsh and strong, bad attitude as he knew the fellow crew members felt, towards the deck hands? Now he was walking out of the cabin leading the way back to the workplace on deck for Jonathon who spoke weakly as they went:

"I don't know how I am going to take charge after hearing this bad news."

The two reached the foray of deckhands who seemed to be waiting for them. Jonathon imagined that he could see smirks on the local's faces. Did they all know his predicament? And was it sneers showing on the lips of the captain and his officers? Unaware of it, a form of paranoia was enveloping him. His legs shook under him.

Jonathon greeted the group with a further unsteady "good morning" his stomach tight with anxiety at his thoughts of the repercussions of Tasha's death on his father and grandfather. He also had a paranoid like fear that the men he would be working with for the rest of the day might be aware of his personal news.

As the day grew on with an icy wind blowing in from the desert coast inland, it became tiring and uncomfortable that made it worse for them all. Jonathon, especially was in the predicament of having no else to share his personal feelings with the disastrous circumstances that he found himself in. He would have liked to have spoken, or confided in Jean his girlfriend from student days right at this time. She would have understood. Now there was only Marijke and her two friends Petronella and Marieta ashore in Cape Town who might just show some kind of female solace towards him in this tragedy.

The day wore on. He was only able as time passed, to offer a blank stare at the deck shift members' questioning him as regards work to be done. This delayed the work pace that the crew hands were trying to keep up with Jonathon. The captain had told him that they must take orders from this young man. So they could not understand Jonathon's lack of attention towards them.

Not only was Jonathon completely nonplussed in the situation with trying to concentrate on the work at hand, the amassing of the ocean bed samples brought up by the dredging basket from the ocean depths. He could also only meet the ever more pointed and irritating questions of the workmen with uncomprehending and time wasting looks, or with a cursory word or two thrown in here and there, as far as his shift crew were concerned.

His mother Tasha was dead. His mind flitted from thoughts of his childhood with his parents when he was growing up. Hadn't Tasha stood out against his coming out to South Africa? This meant conflict had built up in the family situation. Wanting to prolong the danger and excitement that his father had experienced on board the aircraft carriers during the wartime, he had encouraged his son's exploits, against his wife's wishes.

Jonathon felt stuck in the middle of a family conflict. His grandfather, his dear old grandfather had blamed his own wife Alice, his grandmother with her obsessive collecting mania, yes, for Tasha his mother's neurotic behavior. His mind went dull and blank again at yet another harsh question from one of the deck hands as to where Jonathon wanted the latest haulage sediment sample of possible diamond bearing matter from the seabed, to be placed.

Jonathon was on the point of giving up, speaking to the captain and telling him that he could not continue in the employment of the company. Even that would not make sense in his life as his circumstances now were. If he took this course of action there was no doubt that he would have to remain aboard for another five weeks before the next helicopter arrived in the shift crew change.

This would leave him with absolutely nothing to do. His life would then be empty with thoughts of his family and their tragedy flooding over him. No, he decided. The compassionate yokel who had encouraged him to go back on board where he now stood listlessly waiting to give the next order, had given the best, if only, the best advice that he could get.

He raised his head and tried to take in the situation. There were a number of drop baskets being manned to scrape the ocean at its surface. Buckets of sea sand silt stood neatly in a row, ready for the afternoon's analysis process of being checked for diamond bearing sediment. He tried to focus on what the captain had told him about his work routine.

Yes, that was it. Every few days the captain had said the position of the ship as it was lying off the huge estuary of the Orange River on the coast, would have to be mathematically checked by him, taking a sighting as to the angle that the ship was anchored at. The ship the captain had said drifted with the ebb and flow of the tide and the navigating engineers had a continual battle to retain the best anchorage. These thoughts rushed through Jonathon's brain. He grasped at a straw, that there was plenty to keep him busy. In his subconscious he was disturbed by a particularly nasty jolt.

An aggressive looking working crewmember was trying to attract his attention at the moment of his deciding to carry on in the work situation. From what the man was saying, it seemed that he was neglecting his duty. Irritating Jonathon, this person said:

"We have lost one of the drop baskets, meneer. I think that there is a shark in the sea right near, below that is crunching at the metal haulage line. We have tried to pull, but the monster great white shark was too strong for us. What must we do baas?"

Snapping into action Jonathon answered, disregarding the inconvenience of replacing the drop basket and the expense that it would involve to replace it, saying weakly:

"Let it go. The company is wealthy enough to have it put in order again." The man answered curtly:

"Reg, neneer. We does that."

Hunger gnawed at Jonathon's guts as the morning drew to a close and the minutes ticked on to the lunch break. The thought did strike the young man that the food on offer on board was not too bad, quite tasty in fact. Yes, the man who had been a good Samaritan to him upon first tackling the news of his mother's death and coming to grips with it in his thoughts, had been right. He should take his mind off the nastiness of his personal predicament and resume duty as supervisor to the haulage upwards of diamond bearing silt from the ocean bed.

Yes he had been so right! He was feeling better already and at being told about the great white shark in action over the rails of the vessel where the sediment was being heaved up mechanically, began to take an increased interest in the action. He began to think, was it not exciting what he was involved in?

Were not diamonds the world's most precious gem? As hunger struck again, Jonathon desperately sought a motive for living now he was facing the fact that Tasha was gone. His mother was dead. What did it matter how many diamond chips that were in the basket that the man were trying to draw his attention to?

The crewman in question was now saying:

'The great white shark has let go of our haulage basket, sir." Jonathon answered:

"What is that to me? It's your job."

It gave the young man a bit of a lift to see the man cringe slightly at his words. Maybe he ought to be taking the upper hand more in this situation on board. Tasha was dead and gone now. Couldn't he pull himself together? Yes, lunch would probably make the whole future much less bleak. He stared down and then into the distance for a few moments, making sure that the equipment for sighting the ship's ever changing position was where he thought that he had left it. The desert coastline shone gleaming white over the ocean's surface towards land. The air was tangy and brisk. He heard a summons to eat:

"Lunch break, all" It was the galley hand calling them.

At this expected though welcome news, Jonathon gave a sigh of relief, in his supposed superiority in the working situation at seeing that the quota of drop baskets had been hauled up all of them before the midday meal. The very fact that he had kept himself busy if not only physically, as much mentally in the morning's undertakings, gave him a bleak cheerfulness in his subconscious thinking. Someone's loud though surrepticious words trickled into his subconscious thinking: "The food is good lately." Jonathon felt the hairs on his neck rise in the tense pre-lunch situation. Was this another of the crewmembers who was trying to be familiar with him? What was a suitable answer in his position? These people it was quite clear had no idea of the background that he came from. He stopped though in the queue to climb below board into the ship's galley and the thought struck him: did he know on the other hand the sort of background that these crew members came from his own life's point of view to date? His thinking stalled the queue in the rush to get some sustenance. Words again floated into his thinking:

"Kom now baas. All of us is baie honger. Us mus maak gou. Quick now. There is plenty work after the eating. We must hurry."

Jonathon was obviously to them both unaware of the tireless pace of action both aboard ship and even the kind of life that was lived in this country. In his thinking he fled back to the lazy pace of events back in Great Britain. How could folk exist in this flurry and scramble that appeared to be the norm in this employment situation with the company? Finally as Jonathon thought, without breaking their necks they were all pushing and shoving with Jonathon in the fray, to grab a chair each in the galley to eat at table. The galley stewards were nifty and quick in their dishing of the meal and satisfaction with the eating process drew in.

Jonathon again became conscious of the conversation that was ensuing around him. It seemed to involve the political situation in the country of South Africa where he was based. It appeared that he was being addressed by the men in the group of crew hands. At this expected though welcome break Jonathon gave a sigh of relief in his supposed superiority in the working situation of seeing that the quota of drop baskets had been hauled up, all of them before the midday meal and finished for the morning. The very fact that he had kept himself busy if not physically as much as mentally in the morning's undertaking, gave him a bleak cheerfulness in the situation. Someone's words trickled into his subconscious thinking.

"The food is good. Kom, baas. Now we eat."

Immediately Jonathon felt the hairs on his neck rise. Was this another of the crew members who was trying to be familiar with him? What was a suitable answer in his predicament? These people it was quite clear had no idea of the background that he came from. He stopped and just stood in the queue to climb below board into the ship's galley and the thought struck him that did he know on the other hand the sort of background these crew members came from his own point of view? His thinking and stopping had stalled the queue in the rush to get some sustenance. Words again floated into his thinking:

"Kom now baas. All of us is baie honger. Us mus maak gou, be quick. There is plenty work after eating. We must hurry."

Jonathon was obviously to them not aware of the tireless pace of action both aboard ship and even the kind of life that was lived in this country. Everything was new to him. His thinking darted back to the lazy pace of events back in Great Britain. How could folk exist in this flurry and scramble that appeared to be the norm in this employment situation with the company?

Finally as Jonathon thought without breaking his neck they were all pushing and shoving, himself in the fray, to grab a chair in the eating cabin. The galley stewards were nifty and quick in their dishing of the meal as satisfaction with the eating process drew in. Jonathon again became conscious of the conversation that was ensuing around him. It seemed to involve the political situation in the country of South Africa where he was based. It appeared that he was being aggressively addressed by the men in the group of crewhands, and not very pleasantly at that.

The men's voices began to irritate Jonathon. He had not slept well the night before so this and the bad family news that he had received was causing him to fight out a situation with the older crewmen that he was supposed to have charge of. He was feeling light headed and in need of sleep and the constant physical activity of the day was making his bones ache.

He had tried that afternoon to get on with the crewhands, his so called staff, by lifting and carrying the samples of seabed sediment so that if they did start grumbling about his superior rank. That meant that if he did none of the work himself, that the men were doing and he just standing and giving orders, they could not point a finger at him. His temper was becoming short.

The deckhands were, in his opinion after working with them for the whole day seemingly of very coarse stock and breeding. They obviously had no appreciation for any niceties that were being prepared in the galley for supper. Giving him a start in his standing on deck, feeling rather isolated and trying to appear like someone in authority, a piercing whistle like sound came from somewhere above the deck where they were all mustering to go down to the ablution quarters before the meal.

Obviously this was the official signal to stop work for the day. The hands scrambled for the descent ladder to the below deck area. Jonathon, a patient person by nature gathered what was happening but let them all go ahead of him. The men teased and riled one another and as they gathered they saw that Jonathon was holding back. With very little respect for him they began to quip and comment and rile. Jonathon reacted to this behavior that seemed to include him by saying tersely:

"Yes men. Down below now. I'll follow you"

With much scrambling and jesting amongst themselves, sometimes with goodhearted commenting, Jonathon picked up in his now tired and hypersensitive state that was still reeling from the news of Tasha, his mother's death, that they found his being in charge of them most unstable and lacking in guidance. They needed a leader but could see that the young man was much too sensitive for this having as they did tough shipboard experience.

At the comment from one of the more forward and rough looking of the men who spoke gratingly the words: "Is meneer siek. Jou lyk so," Jonathon felt a feeling of faintness coming on. He tried to pull himself together. Was it because of hunger? Finally there was the crush of men needing their meal at the soonest possible time with the strong ozone in the sea air during the day whetting their appetites. They were all physically tired now and weakly after joining in the ablution process there was a scramble for chairs to begin the meal.

Tempting aromas came from the galley kitchen. There was a tension present amongst the men, surreptiously towards Jonathon who took what he supposed to be the superior seat at the head of the long rough wooden table that was chained to the floor to protect a rolling during any possible storm. There was a lull. As any chef would know there were delays in the cooking process and in the waiting process the stewards' part in serving the crew was to get everything under control with fried fish and vegetables chopped that afternoon by the galley hands on the lower deck and already cooked and piping hot. One of them said:

"You men will need something meaty to eat to see you though the ongoing work tomorrow."

The steward was trying to pacify the crew hands' hunger. A discussion started. One of the meaner amongst those seated at table gave a shifty look at Jonathon seated close by.

The ocean was rolling strongly. One of the meaner looking men at the table gave a shifty look at Jonathon seated close by and remarked:

"Its not long before us people are going vote just like you whiteys. They say, the people that everyone in South Africa is going to get a vote in the government that they want.

Egged on by these words, Jonathon still felt his brain still dazed at the news that he had only this morning of Tasha's death and also the effects of the smoking haze at the party in Cape Town that he had now left for shipboard duty. He desperately mustered up sharp words to temper this man's forwardness, trying to control his ever more fragile feelings at the man's probing attitude.

The meal was underway with comments thrown around by the men, surly and snide being increasingly directed at Jonathon the only one of his background that was unfamiliar to them, although under contract they were forced to be under his supervision by the company. Jonathon picked up in the local lingo that the men were aware of a huge political change running on beneath the political regime in South Africa that was holding on to priviledges that were being taken for granted.

This was all expected to change in the next month. Jonathon understood from the conversation that the government was at present undergoing a huge shift of power. The men, discussing this over the meal were grim in their comments. As one of the type of people whose culture had held such people as these contract hands under sway, Jonathon realized that they had been most harshly and cruelly treated. In Jonathon's own personality he felt was weak in comparison to theirs.

He felt that the underhand pointed remarks were being directed at him. He sensed as their superior that he should take an attitude of quelling the rebellious remarks that were being made ever more directed towards him as time went on. Sulkily the nastier of the men spoke to Jonathon directly:

"Ja baas. The time is short. Us people know our job. We is not taking you to lead us if you does not make yourself a strong person to tell us what to do. You is too weak to control here. Us cannot work like that. We will make a man from us deck hands to control the work tomorrow. The captain will let it go. He knows that he can depend on us. What does he, the captain do anyway but smoke and drink in his cabin."

The man was becoming insolent towards Jonathon. They would not understand the delicate state of his thinking and current shock in his family situation. He felt vulnerable with not a soul to confide in. He pulled himself up: better not to look for sympathy and pull himself together. Jean back in Great Britain, he thought in the moment, would have agreed with this decision.

Even though he felt insulted as a person not even having any birth ties with this country and being spoken to like this he felt a surge of pride at being part of this great change that was taking place in the land. He felt nothing in common with these folk that he was forced by company contract to be with on board this diamond dredging barge. He had been given a role of superiority in a situation that clearly had not been properly investigated as running smoothly in the male issues social sense.

These people who were rebelliously taking control in the circumstances were his inferiors and he understood that he should in the critical situation take control of matters. He quickly pulled this thoughts together in trying to concentrate on what was being said ever more angrily by the men he was eating the meal with. No, he must not think of Tasha. That part of his life was over. He would never see her again. Life at this moment was something that he must decide on what to do.

Thinking that the men did not notice his feeling of tension and fear at the aggression that they were showing and trying to understand why they were behaving in this disjointed way he spoke sharply:

"You men have no right to treat me like this. Your jobs will be taken away from you if you treat me like this."

Then Jonathon having said this all he could muster up for the moment, felt utterly pathetic. Then having made this verbal reaction he understood that he had at least put on some sort of show of authority over them all. Coarse muttering ensued from them becoming louder as the moments ticked by. The nastiest of the group as he had pinpointed amongst them all, pushed back his chair roughly and obviously riled and with no self control, slowly felt inside his jacket. Jonathon watched him rise from his chair out of the corner of his eye.

Then the man moved swiftly over to him. Jonathon suddenly saw that he was holding a knife in his hand. The man in what seemed to Jonathon an instantaneous movement took him by the shoulder and held the knife to Jonathon's throat saying:

"This is what you will get if you do not listen to us. Us knows the work to do here on this boat. Us do not have to listen to a person like you. You knows nothing. But we will teach you."

Jonathon felt his eyes bulge in his head. He tried to edge his head away from the man's grip that was now hurting him. At the shock of the situation Jonathon at first could not think clearly. The point of the knife pressed into his skin and he gradually began to summon up words to bring matters under control. He spoke knowing that this assailant could not possibly with all the other men seated at the super table, do anything more violent than this threatening act.

Like a flash the reason for the action this man was taking went through his mind. People like this had enough more than they could take from folk of Jonathon's culture, or at least what he seemed to be to them. They did not realize that he was from Great Britain. They did not discern that he and the captain and officers were of totally different backgrounds socially.

They merely considered him a weakling, ever more so he thought, with having lost his mother Tasha in the present circumstances. His workmates muttered support in taking out on him this cruel treatment people such as they had been receiving from men like the captain and his henchmen. Jonathon was being lumped together with the dominant people in the country, as a scapegoat.

The point of the knife eased from his throat. Perhaps it was because he had made no movement of retaliation that the man's aggression was being staved off. The person said:

"You understand now baas? Us does not like it that you tell us our jobs will go. Very soon it is people like you who will do this heavy work. Us know our jobs. Us do not need people like you."

The whole matter became a culture clash. Footsteps could be heard outside the galley door. Everyone in the cabin tensed. Quickly the assailant put his knife back in the inside of his jacket. Weakly Jonathon thought, still worse for wear from the smoke haze of two nights ago when he had been involved in the party where marijuana had been smoked, here was some support. But was his job at stake now? He felt cornered. He could not tell the captain or officers what had transpired within the last fifteen minutes for fear of being victimized.

Chapter 9

The work crew were eyeing one another shiftily wondering whether Jonathon was going to let on about the drama that had just ensued. It would have caused trouble for them all if that was what he chose to do. Gradually the scraping one the metal floor of the chairs they had all been sitting on became louder and louder, piercing Jonathon's ears. The tension of the occurrence made worse now with the entrance of the Captain and officers caused him to remain immobile in the situation even though the men who had taunted him were now leaving one by one as they edged passed the ship's officials leaving to discuss the incident in the recreation cabin nearby.

The Captain and officers after their drinking bout a while earlier were now needing their meal. It was customary that they ate after the younger grew hands had finished. But Jonathon was still sitting at the table in a dazed fashion. The Captain spoke, a little put out at this display of lack of confidence from this person who was a necessary part of the ship's workings:

"And you meneer? Are you not finished eating too? You must go now. There is a long evening to come. There is darts and snooker in the recreation room that you can do. Or maybe you need to prepare for tomorrow in your cabin."

The Captain in saying this only had a vague idea of what Jonathon had to do in his marine mathematical and analyzing work aboard but did know he was an important member of the crew. Right at that moment though he took in the somewhat helpless state of this person but could not understand why. He spoke again:

"Finish now meneer."

The Captain's voice was strident now. Jonathon was edged hastily out of his seat by the man's words and then came a little to his senses in the situation, mumbling out the words:

"Yes. Yes sir. I must also leave now. Of course. I am going out of the galley now."

Urgently the thought struck him that he must under no circumstances tell his superiors what had just happened at the eating table. In his uneasy and confused state of mind he tried to focus. He was unsteady on his feet because of the ocean rocking the diamond mining barge, ever more jolting him as the night gale outside over the sea made the vessel sway heavily.

Jonathon with his head lowered in shock awkwardly rose up from his seat hands flaying around him as he tried to find his balance. The captain and officers neared him needing to take their place to be served in the supper meal. Jonathon, curiously as far as the Captain was concerned stumbled towards the door of the galley. Having been imbibing and smoking they also were in a somewhat unsteady frame of mind, also being hungry.

They swayed their way in Jonathon's direction. Step by step out of the door and down the gangway the young man felt his way to his cabin berth.

He could scarcely remember where he was headed for. On reaching his sleeping quarters, he flung himself down on the cabin bunk, scarcely able to think. Lying there gradually his thoughts began to focus. Most definitely he would have to leave this ship's captain and crew situation. It would be a war of nerves if he had to stay and work with these people after what had happened. The whole incident might just come out and even then the working tension would be unbearable. But he was contracted into the situation aboard for the next six weeks. He tried to clear his thoughts and think urgently for a solution, a way and means to get out of all this.

He had closed his eyes but now opened them in an effort to face reality. All that he could see was the torn picture poster stuck on the cabin was of a hot number of a rather loose looking woman, the color in the photograph fading. The sight depressed him as he suddenly thought of Jean. Yes. He must somehow get back to her and leave this awful situation. But how to do it? The wind was howling outside and whipping up the motion of the barge. In his desperation he fell asleep off and on for about three or four hours. Then he came awake. His mind was now quite clear. The wind outside had stilled and the ocean swells much less. The minor storm was abating.

Off and on during the night Jonathon half dozed and was half awake. He fought in his mind the necessity for leaving the situation that had been created around his presence aboard. Not only was he experiencing violence from the crew workers that had come to the point of being unmanageable for him but also verbal riling from the Captain and his officials.

As he tensed and relaxed in sleep as the night went on he noticed the rolling of the barge easing as the heavier ocean swells lessened. This must mean that the weather was going to be clearer when the sun rose. Exhausted from the poor sleep during the night Jonathon had an inspiration in the early hours as he lay awake in desperation at having to face the day.

The ocean being almost still outside and without any wind being audible he made up his mind in a final conclusion to battle out the circumstances that he found himself in. That was it! His mind snapped into reality. He would jump ship just as soon as it was light. He had noticed that the ship was lying not too far off the desert coastline and he could recall seeing some buildings ashore in the not to far distance. That meant there were people who could help him get back to Cape Town. Yes! It was bravado yes, but he would swim to freedom.

In the potential danger of the plan his thoughts became urgent and muddled especially with the poor night's sleep in the last ten hours and the residue of the smoke haze of the party in Cape Town a couple of night's ago. The air in the early morning was chill but he realized in his plan to swim ashore that he would have to discard the jersey that he had donned the night before over the fairly light clothing that he had slept in.

As his hand brushed his pants in pulling off the jersey he became aware of a stony lump deep in the pocket of his clothing. It pressed into his body uncomfortably and in his haste and irritation he pulled it out, wondering what it was. Then he saw wrapped in plastic that it was a sea sand encrusted rough diamond. His heart pumped both at finding it and what he was planning to do. The stone had obviously been planted on him to cause further trouble for him with the Captain. It had been made to seem as if he had stolen a company possession. Carelessly and not thinking too much about it at that minute, he put the stone back into his pocket.

Then he had to unwrap the sand encrusted stone again. It had been one of thousands that the hardy crewmen dredged up every month from the ocean bed. Clearly their antagonism towards his weakened taking of authority had increased now that he had been radioed of the suicide of his mother, that was unbeknown to the crew on board. It was obvious that some of the men had spitefully placed this rough encrusted diamond stone in his pocket in the hope that he would be found out as having stolen it for his own gain.

Then in their thinking he would lose his job if found on him. Or so they thought. Jonathon in his overactive mind from poor sleep that night, in the early hours thought that he was not going to let these people get the better of him. He had wrapped the stone but again took it out and stared at it. This was out and out malice being enacted towards him. He decided angrily that he would get the better of them in his plan to jump ship in the next couple of hours, with the planted gem still on his person, just after the sun had risen.

Grimly he perceived that that the heavy swells of the night before had abated and the sea was quite calm with only gentle swelling of movement over the side of the deck. He had staggered down the gangway and he had climbed the ladder to aboveboard having now left his cabin. This would mean that fortune was on his side in his positive purpose of abandoning the tension that the threat of the knifing him the night before had caused by attempting to swim, god knew how across the stretch of ocean to the desert shore that in his shattered judgment did not seem too far away. The early morning light that hit his eyes gradually dazzled his vision as the first rays of the sun lit up the purple sky on the desert horizon. In his desperation and anxiety as well his ever increasing lack of correct estimation of what he was capable of in his effort to ease the unbearable tension that he hoped to leave by jumping overboard. He felt forced to leave by this only means possible.

Jonathon walked uneasily up and down the deck near the space in the railings that was used to pull up the dredging baskets full of possible diamond bearing silt. The sun was gradually becoming brighter and brighter as it rose over the desert horizon the purple sky of earlier becoming a rosy orange. Jonathon was becoming anxious in suddenly realizing the potential danger of his plan to escape.

The white shore in the distance suddenly seemed so much further away than he had reckoned on in his intentions while lying on his cabin bunk the night before. He suddenly doubted what he had wanted to do. But he was cornered now. If he did not jump ship and swim for it he would be left with ongoing and unbearable tension aboard the diamond dredger. He racked his brains for a solution.

Was it not possible to approach the Captain, or at least one of the officers in command of the vessel and inform them of what had happened with the ugly threat of the knife being held to his throat the night before? No, he could not do it. It would just cause more dislike and enmity. Anyway not only was he held in scorn by the working crew already, but he had felt that he was also disliked by the senior officials on board because he was not of their sort of person. No, he was from another land. Not like them.

The sun was nearly blinding him now. His heart was pumping fast as he stared down into the ocean below. He thought briefly that it was to his advantage that his clothing was light. He looked around. There was nobody in the immediate vicinity of where he was standing. But he had not looked upwards at the navigating cabin above the deck. He had not seen the officer on night watch inside.

This person had spotted him but was not unduly worried for the moment. That was until he saw the young man looking down at the swelling of the waters below the space in the ship's railings. He did not know that Jonathon had made an instantaneous decision. The sea flowing below to him was freedom from this unbearable forced situation aboard.

While all these thoughts were running through the mind of the officer on watch, there began action down below on deck with the figure of Jonathon. The officer's attention was gradually becoming conscious of the drama below. As he watched two items came to his attention as the night watch's duty was.

He was on the point of switching on the sea to land emergency radio dialing frequency. He had the air wave number at his fingertips as he had been trained. To his horror even in the job that he been chosen for he saw the young man take a running dive off the stern of the diamond dredger. His heart pumping he cowered anxiously over the radio set. The crackling became instantaneously clearer by the second. Then in a state of high tension the officer spoke into the receiver:

"Calling air watch Namibia. Calling air watch Namibia." He repeated these words twice again. Further crackling came through the airwaves this time obviously directed at the ship's watch, within seconds. The officer's heart raced. Had he been quick enough? Yes. A voice came through the radio waves to him, clipped and urgent.

"Air station Namibia. Air station Namibia. Receiving. Receiving. Query reason of call out. Query reason for call out."

The officer aboard was now in full attention and prided himself in answering the response:

"Man overboard. Man overboard."

Crackling ensued from the radio set as he waited once again for a response. In two or three seconds the reply came through:

"Urgent. Urgent. Direct flight incoming to the area of crisis near ship." The officer had clearly seen Jonathon's dive into the sea at the stern from the cabin up top, so was able immediately to answer over the radio static that was interfering irritatingly:

"Area of emergency to the stern. Direct flight to the ocean at stern of ship. Man overboard. Man overboard to stern. Man overboard to stern."

He repeated himself nearly panicking even though as the trained official that he was aboard. Suddenly there was silence but only for another five seconds. Then the same clipped tense voice came over:

"Flight takeoff within fifteen seconds." The voice repeated itself. What more could the officer on board do but weakly though audibly confirm and respond:

"Message received. Message received. Awaiting help here. Awaiting help here."

Jonathon had tried in his nervous pacing up and down at the stern of the vessel to make his final decision of the action of jumping off into the sea. He did not realize that he was being covertly watched by the officer on duty. He also did not realize that what he was about to do could be taken to mean that was attempting suicide.

This in his thinking at the time, was not the case at all. He had no intention of committing suicide and as the later events in the circumstances to follow came to light it was an act of youthful ignorance of the dangers involved. He had every thought and wish at the moment when he finally flung himself off the stern into the sea, of escaping the frightening tensions aboard of the knife wielding crew member the night before. He wanted to make every attempt that he was able to swim to land.

Desperately as his body members flayed in all directions as he fell through the air he thought that this must be possible. The ocean below became nearer and nearer in his sight. He had the double experience of feeling free now but afraid of what he had done. It seemed like forever that he was swaying through the air. It was still early in the morning and the light of the sun's rays did little to warm him.

Then with an icy jolt he hit the water underneath him. At first the severe chill of the sea took his breath away completely. He found himself moving his arms and legs desperately to keep himself afloat. He was not even aware of what was now the great ship that he had just left. The ocean swelled and sucked at his body. For the first few minutes he was able to keep his head out of the water but then had the terrifying feeling of being sucked under and having to keep his mouth shut to avoid being overcome by swallowing the salt water. He looked up and down then summoning up all his strength to keep afloat. He had no idea that this would be so difficult, even as the giant swells sucked at him.

Then as he felt an intermittent drumming sound inside his head and thinking as this sound came into his hearing, he began to imagine think what it was like to drown in the sea. He had not thought about what it would be like if he could not swim to shore as had seemed so easy, this plan of escape. This roaring sound, was this the end of his life? He became then anxious and desperate in the situation. Yes, it must mean that he was up against his death moment. Yes, he thought in shock. This must be it, the end of everything that he had ever known.

He had, even before running off the deck of the diamond mining dredger that he was now regretting, found that at least it had been a place of temporary safety. In the wet and icy chill of the waters sucking at him, he had forgotten the feeling of the residue of the smoke haze from the party of the night before and the terror that he had felt at being threatened at knifepoint last evening at supper. All this had gone out of his mind and all he could feel were his clothes clinging to his body and the hopeless flailing of his arms trying as he had planned over the near sleepless night before, to start his swim to shore

Then suddenly in the reality of what was happening it was clear that his plan was now impossible. The rolling giant wave swells sucked at his body and each time it lifted him, then the swell receded pulling him under, under. He sent up one last desperate prayer. Then he heard approaching him and nearing from a distance another roaring sound, from a distance but getting nearer. It was different from the sound he had been experiencing in his head in the danger of his plight and was coming closer and closer.

It was coming from above. He could just hear with the seawater clogging his ears. He knew that a helicopter had brought he and the crewmen to the desert coast but was not aware that the great chopper had remained on standby near the sprinkling of human dwellings that it had taken off from to lift the men onto the ship. Was this a chance of help? Somehow to get out of this danger in the sea? His heart thumped. Yes it was.

Then the helicopter was hovering over him and he could hear men shouting faintly from right up above. Jonathon in his near hopeless plight of trying to stay afloat in the up and down pulling of the ocean wave swells managed to raise his head a few times over the surface of the water to grasp the fact in his mind that hope was at hand.

Inside the helicopter now hovering nearby reaching the ocean area where the rescuers were trying to do their duty to help this person in distress the men were grimly trying to communicate in their effort to help. The door to the cabin connecting the pilot to the two others who were going to help pull the distressed man up to the aircraft, was open. The two rescuers were preparing to throw down a tough and hardy rope to with a sturdy handle at the end. Words came over to these two men from the pilot's cabin:

"Are we right over the ocean stern area? I cannot see over the nose of the chopper into the sea. As we were approaching I spotted the man in distress but I think from my judgment that we are almost directly above the person in the water now. Am I correct? Guide me, guide me, please, frontwards and backwards and sideways."

The more quickly responding of the two men dared to go to the side open area of the helicopter, even though the aircraft was swaying in it's hovering. It seemed nearly in vain. The would-be rescuer knew that he must respond to the pilot the leader of the operation. He shouted, as this was the only way of being heard over the drumming of the ship's engine, the roar of the ocean and the noise of the motors of the helicopter itself. Fortunately the pilot caught his words but only faintly. He replied:

"Hold steady, hold steady as we go. The person in distress is right below. We are throwing the rope down now."

Words in response came from the pilot's cabin:

"I can hold steady now, but only at most for another three quarters of an hour. That is the limit with the fuel available to get safely back."

At these words the two men uncoiled the rope of rescue and grimly in fear of their own safety hurled down the rope, holding on to the side of the helicopter as they did so to prevent their own falling out. After five minutes they felt a tug at the rope. One of the men said to the other:

"He's holding on, he's holding on. I can't see over the side, but now we must pull him up now." The pilot answered:

"Holding, holding. Action now as quick as possible."

Then began Jonathon's slowly being hauled upwards into the chopper. His soaked and distraught person was slowly pulled upwards and into the safety of the inside of the helicopter. He was breathing heavily and it seemed to him that his arms and shoulders were being pulled out of their sockets at the pressure from the haulage from above in the air.

He had tried about three times to catch hold of the rope end. Fortunately he was young and reasonably fit. So in a final grabbing of the rope end and the jerk of being pulled out of the water at one of the upwards surging waves of the swelling sea the worst of the long journey on the rope end was accomplished.

Then it was up to both the rescuers and the rescued. Now he was out of the seawater. He had a sturdy frame and did not carry too much extra weight so the rescuers had realized. It seemed that the chances were good for Jonathon's survival in the dramatic ordeal. He could not see into the interior of the helicopter but knew that there were people inside who were helping him.

As the men aboard the chopper felt the burden of the person whose life they were saving lessen, they knew that he could hear them so they shouted down out of the hovering aircraft. Before trying to make verbal contact to Jonathon who was hanging from the rope now close below the man in charge of the operation called to the pilot:

"How much longer have we got in fuel time?"

It seemed that they had been hauling the body upwards for an age, so long that they had lost track of time. The men were tiring quickly now. The pilot caught their words and answered:

"We have one quarter of an hour to go. One quarter of and hour to go. Will you make it, getting the man aboard the chopper or must we abandon hope? Answer please."

The brighter of the two men responded

"Mission successful. Hold steady. Hold steady. Man aboard aircraft within five minutes." Then Jonathon's head appeared at the side of the chopper. He was gasping for breath and desperate after the ordeal and of course dripping wet in the still very cold early hours of the morning, off the icy desert Namibian coast.

With one last frantic heave upwards both on the part of the rescuers who were pulling up the rope with Jonathon holding on at the end bar of the hand grip, they had him inside the chopper with no more than a few cuts and grazes to his arms and legs in scraping himself on the side of the metal side opening of the helicopter. The two men were feeling great emotion for the ordeal that Jonathon had just experienced, no less themselves in the danger of tumbling out of the open side. One of them said, nearly losing control of himself:

"Take it easy. Take it easy. We've got you here. We've got you up."

They could all scarcely breathe a sigh of relief. On seeing how Jonathon was shivering fit to collapse the men as trained for this sort of eventuality that only happened once in a lifetime, pulled a large army style blanket around the unfortunate young man. As they did so Jonathon felt a pressing and scraping of a hard object against his thigh. Although he was hardly in his senses he tried to think clearly in the rough rubbing dry that the rescuers were doing for him. They were trying to get his body blood circulation going again after his icy dip in the sea. What was it hurting his thigh, he wondered.

Then he was vaguely conscious of the reason in the memory gap between the last evening and the present time. He realized dimly but urgently in his mind that it was the small sand-encrusted diamond stone had been obviously planted the night before on his person in the pocket of his clothing that he had put out to wear today. This very unclear realization increased his anxiety in the situation he was in because he did not want more of having to assert himself with any authority in the matter. He remembered his increasingly weak minded attitude in keeping control in his job aboard ship after hearing about Tasha his mother's suicide. That was in the short time that it had lasted.

So dimly and vaguely he made a mental note to keep the diamond in his personal care, unknown to anyone until he reached a place of independence. That would be seemingly first to a place of safety on land from aboard the helicopter and then on to the boarding house in Cape Town. He could not see any more into the future after that, but had it in mind to somehow reach the shelter of his grandfather's Great House in Great Britain eventually.

Chapter 10

Jonathon had never felt so bad. Everything seemed hopeless and he could not get to grips with the fact that the crisis was over. He could only sense the reality of feeling nearly sick with cold and discomfort. A voice came through from seemingly nowhere but it was the pilot's warning the three passengers on board that they were heading for land and further circumstances in Jonathon's life. The words came through: "Rising! Rising!"

With the added feeling of his stomach churning in the swaying of the chopper as its rotors carried them all upwards into a line of flight directed to the sprinkling of habitations near the sea, but on the edge of the never ending desert. There the pilot had taken off from in his mission of mercy after the emergency summons from the diamond dredger anchored off the coastal desert.

The men clutched all railings inside the aircraft, grasping at Jonathon to keep him steady. They could see that he desperately needed a seat. There were only two cramped places to sit so Jonathon was pushed into one of them, a little dryer now but still shivering uncontrollably in the icy interior of the metal built chopper.

Not only was the air freezing in the early morning but outside an early morning mist was playing over the coast coming from the south as the sun rose gradually higher. Still there seemed no way of keeping warm despite the sun's rays flickering in and out of the interior of the chopper at both sides. The pilot's voice came through the door of the nose of the helicopter:

"Hold steady as we go. Hold steady. We're going down now. We're landing in ten minutes. Hold tight, hold tight you all. Tell the survivor we'll have him in hospital within just over half an hour." With the jolting about Jonathon even began to fear a safe landing.

Then the pilot could be heard speaking over the radio to the ship out at sea:

"Mission accomplished. Mission accomplished." Then again the muffled words over the roar of the rotors outside:

"Coming in to land. Are you ready?" Obviously some sort of radio landing guidance was awaiting them. Again Jonathon with a last gulp of grasping what freedom he had made for himself after the tension aboard ship, heard the pilot's words:

"Are you ready to receive us?" He was again addressing the land based radio set up. Then with a cacophony of static the men felt a tremendous jolt. The helicopter was finally on the makeshift gravel landing strip.

No sooner out of the helicopter than with the towel still wrapped around him Jonathon was hustled into a small clean building. At the entrance an efficient looking young woman met the incoming group. She said briskly addressing Jonathon in particular as the person in distress as she could see.

"So you are the survivor in this sea drama. Your name is Jonathon you say? We will have you in a warm bed with plenty of blankets immediately." She gestured to the men saying:

"It's all right now. We will take over, the resident doctor and I. Come this way Jonathon."

The rescuers turned to leave. Now a hospital patient he was left alone with the nurse as they walked down a short corridor and entered a sun filled room with three beds in it made up with heavy blanketing. The sun was streaming into what passed for a hospital ward in this isolated venue in the desert miles from anywhere.

There was a set of sleepwear put out on a chair beside the bed and the nurse said:

"I will show you the bathroom where you can put on this warm clothing and then its straight to bed. You seem to be suffering from extreme exposure. Our doctor will have a name in medical terms for this but meanwhile from what I can see you desperately need warmth in a thickly blanketed bed.

She led the way off to a bathroom on the side of the small room and shut the door while Jonathon changed. He was shaking so that he could scarcely manage. His heart raced as he remembered after all this even, that the sand crusted diamond was still on his person. The nurse looked on curiously as in a jittery fashion he removed the little gem from the wet garment's pocket. Wanting to get him to bed as quickly as possible she was slightly irritated by this preoccupation of her patient and she questioned sharply:

"Is that a personal possession of yours or shall I just throw it away? It looks like some sort of stone. Do you really want to keep it?"

Stuttering in his extreme distress Jonathon just managed to find the words:

"No . . . no . . . no . . . just a container for it. I must . . . . must . . . must . . . keep hold of it." Desperately he hoped that she would question him no further about the little diamond that Jonathon knew for sure had been spitefully planted on him to victimize him should this be found out by the company officials. He did not realize how innocent he was in the circumstances and what a pathetic attempt by the ship's crew this was to nail him as a thief. The nurse said again:

"I'll find an old plastic jar with a lid that you can put it in."

She did not see that it was sand clinging on the little gem that was glinting in Jonathon's direction as he had placed it on the side table in the now strongly sunlit ward. The nurse made her exit after seeing that Jonathon was comfortable and warmer. She said in preparation to the doctor's presence for treating Jonathon according to his condition:

"We suspect that you are suffering from hypothermia from the plunge into the sea. We are not certain why this has happened but the doctor will talk to you about that. You are an unexpected arrival here and it is apparent that you have been unbelievably lucky to have survived your ordeal. We sometimes get army cases up from the training base down south in the little town of Swakopmund but we have little to keep us busy usually.

In this area anything can happen and we are only too happy to help you through the ordeal. It seems to me that you had a reason to tumble overboard from the ship anchored out at sea. You do not seem the usual sort of person that we get here at all."

Having lain there in an iota of comfort in the warmth of the hospital bed Jonathon muttered:

"All I know is that I threw myself off the ship where I was working. I am actually British. For the moment I can't remember why I did this."

He stuttered out these words. Just then the door to the ward opened and a somewhat older man, the doctor appeared with a stethoscope around his neck. He could see a conversation was in process and edged his way into the situation by saying:

"Warm enough? Have you told nurse here what happened?" Jonathon quailed at this curiosity being shown in the circumstances. He did not want to let out why he was there. The doctor tried to get to the bottom of the reason for Jonathon's presence. He started the easy way. It was clearly in his medical training a very suspicious reason for what had happened to the young man having been overboard from the diamond dredger in the sea. He stared curiously at the little plastic bottle that stood on the small side cupboard next to the bed and enquired:

"Is that something you have brought with you?"

Jonathon did not rise to the bait. He did not think at the time that the doctor attending him was being over inquisitive. He just felt in his dire circumstances that this was another human being close by who was showing some positive interest in him. He did not realize at the time the trouble that had been caused for him both by his own action, and the attitude that his parents had taken towards him in his acceptance of this job of work. Now as he was coming to realize as he lay shivering under the doctor's stern but concerned eye, it was developing into huge confusion.

Tasha's death by suicide was just another blackening out in his already troubled emotions. The doctor said persevering, but a little more sympathetically:

"Why were you in the sea Jonathon?"

Jonathon immediately clamped up. He felt there might be even more trouble caused for him if he told of the knife attack. He had not even told any of the officers on board ship about that. It was a personal horror that he would have to live with all the rest of his life. The doctor again spoke:

"I can see that at the moment that you are extremely uncomfortable. We will give you an injection to calm you and take away the tension in the fright and shivering that you are experiencing."

Jonathon was unable to speak. The doctor waited in case Jonathon responded but when he did not, the man turned and as he did the nurse approached with a syringe. Jonathon just lay there in terror but when the treatment was over within half an hour he began to feel more relaxed. His mind and thinking became clearer and he became fully conscious that he was safe maybe only just at present, but more importantly that he was out of the tension situation aboard the diamond dredging ship.

He could only think in the present. The day heated up outside as he heard seagulls mewing in the distance as his body temperature gradually rose. The nurse offered a hot drink from time to time and sandwiches, but Jonathon felt that he could not even eat that day.

Jonathon remained in the little hospital for several days feeling very young and vulnerable. He was too immature to understand the implications of what he had let himself in for. The doctor who saw him from time to time gave him some counseling in the suffering that he was gradually coming through. As he improved the carer said a few days later:

"You will be well advised to see a psychiatrist when you get back to Cape Town There is some doubt about the fact that you tried to take your own life or not." Jonathon tensed again at these words, and replied hardly audibly:

"That's not true, sir." The doctor took in this reply, but continued:

"A motor ride as been arranged in a few days to transport you back to Cape Town to your lodgings. It seems unclear at this time what steps are going to be taken by your employers in the diamond mining company, whether you will be kept on or not."

Jonathon tensed at these words. Would he be left without payment or a job when he reached Cape Town by car within next week? He would have to contact Marijke at her flat and ask for her help if necessary, financial aid and the arranging for a possible return to Great Britain. He wondered if she would be able to contact his father for help. A shock went through his system on the last day in the hospital when the doctor said:

"I think you are better now. One more night to make sure and then its on your way back to Cape Town. Do your feel ready to face the world outsides now?"

Jonathon had been weakly ready but was now more eager to release himself from the situation completely. He had hoped for the glamorous diamond mining job to last, but the reality was that there seemed to have been an undercurrent of complete corruption in his time so far in South Africa. It had all been so completely out of his control.

He began to wonder what the repercussions from the board of directors of the company would be towards him. He felt afraid of having to face his employers in that the whole story of the knife attack might come out. He stared at the plastic jar that the nurse had brought him, containing the rough sand encrusted diamond gem that he had discovered in his pocket after his attempt at jumping ship. No he would not even mention its presence on his person to anyone. It would just complicate matters.

Finally the minute and hour came by when Jonathon was packed and ready to go. His time in the daily sunny ward had been a necessary pleasant time after a rough start there. He turned from the nurse's presence and glanced at the now made up ward bed that he was leaving. At his mild regret the nurse spoke:

"Come now Jonathon. The two company officials who will be escorting you back to Cape Town are waiting in the parking area outside. I have been asked to take you to them to finish my part in this drama."

She gestured to Jonathon to go ahead of her. Outside there was a sea mist playing in the early morning shadows on the coast where Jonathon had been hospitalized. Sunlight filtered through but Jonathon was grateful for the warm jacket on loan to him from the hospital. Suddenly he was in close quarters with two quite shabbily dressed men one of whom addressed Jonathon:

"Are you Mister Jonathon Albany? The one who was working on the dredger offshore out there?" The man glanced seawards.

Jonathon was not too put off by the two men as they did not seem to want, at the present time to cause him any trouble. From what he could see they seemed very South African in the type of person he was coming to judge from his experiences here so far in this country. He was not going to let on any more of his circumstances at the moment. He would play a waiting game with them. He was aware that there was a long haul with them ahead by car. He knew that Africa was a country of vast distances so he said curtly:

"Yes. Yes I am due to travel with you by car through to Cape Town today. Have you any idea who will be contacting me in Cape Town?"

The men spoke together. They obviously did not know any more about what was happening than Jonathon did. One of them addressed him:

"You can get into the car. Is that all you have with you?"

The man indicated the tightly closed plastic container that Jonathon was carrying. Jonathon tensed at this question, all his experiences aboard ship flooding back into his mind so he replied:

"Just something of mine I'm taking back to Cape Town with me."

This was one up on the two men by Jonathon, and the man stood back, impressed at his tone of voice. But the two had a job to do.

Jonathon had managed to fob off the man's question. At least he had managed to pull himself together more assertively in answering the curious question of one of the two men who would be accompanying him in the traveling back to Cape Town in this rather older than most looking car that he had been asked to get into in the totally isolated and unexpected turn of events. He got in and the driver moved off.

In his uncertainty with a slight feeling of paranoia Jonathon tried to think how either of the two men could know anything about him. There could have been no communication from the crew hands aboard ship that he had worked with. They would not have known that the sea sand encrusted rough gem had stayed on his person in this ordeal. Neither would the helicopter pilot or crew have known anything about it. He had also managed to put off any questioning from the nurse and doctor in the hospital.

Although yes, the nurse had been very inquisitive about it but because she was female and young had not been able to put two and two together and realize that it was a sand encoated diamond gem inside the container. No she had just done her duty and found him an item for the keepsake to be put in.

As the car raced along the road through the desert Jonathon began to wonder just what he was going to do with it. He would have to keep it quiet that he was retaining it with his personal belongings. He could not let out this secret in case he was blamed for stealing in the course of duty in the now past experience aboard ship.

Yes, he thought to himself grimly that is just what had been intended in the sneaky and underhand act or planting the little stone in his pocket during the night after the attack on him with a knife. The car raced on. The men stopped talking and Jonathon began to feel lethargic with the boredom of the ride through the desert morning and fell asleep.

About two hours later he drowsily awoke and felt a kind of much needed security in the comfort of his seat in the back of the car. They were traveling on an open road at quite a speed. Jonathon wondered what had awoken him. Then he realized that it was because the two men in the front seats were conversing. He just caught the driver's words.

"Mileage in the hundreds now. We should be reaching the bridge over the Orange river within the next hour."

What else had they been saying before he had awoken? The other man had probably asked him about the progress made in their journey back to Cape Town. The same man asked the driver gruffly:

"Will we be stopping at O'Kiep for something to eat?"

Needing to concentrate the driver took his time in replying.

"Yes," he said. "We will need a rest break and something to eat." At these words Jonathon felt a little eased but was now in his waking state feeling stabs of paranoia with the circumstances he was involved in. Neither of the men had introduced themselves to him by name so he felt somewhat isolated and did not dare to say anything. He pondered as he watched the desert fly by outside the car window. What would happen when he reached his lodgings in Cape Town?

The doctor had spoken of his need to see a psychiatrist. He tried hard to assert himself in his thoughts. This was not fair. Why should he have to have anything to do with all this? But Tasha had warned him not to go to sea. She had told him to take a land based job. And Tasha his beloved mother was dead. Suicide. Shock waves again raced through his body.

The doctor in the little hospital he had just recently left had made him doubt whether his jumping ship had been an act of taking his own life on his part. The boredom of the journey was making him confused in his thinking. Nothing to do as they rode on. No, he had not wanted to end his life by drowning. He had wanted to swim to shore and evade the tense atmosphere aboard the diamond dredger.

So what was his goal and plan of action on reaching the boarding house in Cape Town now? He wondered what the young Dutch girl would have to say when he told her what had happened. Yes, of all the consequences of being an employee on the diamond barge dredger off the coast of south west Africa, he knew that he had to confide in someone and this girl Marijke was the closest he could come to someone connected to his own family. Hadn't Tasha now dead, given her his father's telephone number? Wasn't she someone at least from the same part of the world in the northern hemisphere? Her parents were Dutch Embassy contacts. He remembered. Yes wasn't that near Great Britain where his grandfather was? That was safety to aim at in this ordeal.

She would at least take a matter of fact interest in the horrors that had been occurring in his life. Then he fell asleep again with the journey calming him, only to be awoken at the likelihood of something to eat. They had reached the little town of O'Kiep on the their way back to Cape Town. Jonathon was not really hungry but had the sense to swallow down a couple of sandwiches. Not much was said at the stop at the little copper mining town. Their arrival caused a slight stir amongst the locals. It was obvious not many travelers came this way. Then they came en route again Jonathon tiring increasingly as the journey approached its end. He awoke to what he observed in his two fellow travelers in the car, was for them quite stimulated chat. Courtesy of the company the automobile escorting Jonathon was slowing slightly. The lights of Cape Town beckoned. One of the men spoke directly to the driver: "Yes up this road. The long way round into town. Yes I know it's a detour but it's safer this way. The driver spoke bad temperedly now:

"We have only got less than a sixth of a tank full of petrol left." The other responded:

"Spin it out then brother. We have to get this man back to his lodgings by night. There's nothing else we can do with him."

The unease of not really knowing the two filtered again into Jonathon's thinking. Again he felt part of an ongoing drama in which he was being used. He was being ignored in fact. He was not being asked for any opinion about the ongoing circumstances that he was finding himself in. Then again did he want anyone to know? They were not even speaking to him. He felt a little insulted.

He knew what his grandfather would have thought of them in their insolent attitude. But now he was at the company's mercy. They had brought him, as the car drew up to a place he recognized the boarding house he had left for this while, to where there was a bed to doss down for the night.

He was suddenly in the situation where he would have to plan what to do next. He must contact Marijke. He hoped that she would still be in Cape Town. She had seemed those few days ago after the horrendous events still to be very much involved with her student friends and himself here. She at least had a car. He hoped she would not involve him in any more parties after the last one's disastrous effects.

Fear hit him. What attitude were his employers going to take? In the innocence of youth he did not realize the trouble that he was in. His thoughts rose to a consciousness of the outside events taking place. The driver muttered aggressively, tired now after the long ride from the hospital in Namibia.

"Here is the boarding house."

Slowly a glimmer of hope filtered dimly into Jonathon's thinking. It would be a temporary haven. He stumbled out of the car in the warmth of the Cape summer evening. He stared uncertainly at the men. Were there any more formalities to undergo? The driver just said to him:

"This is the right place where you are staying."

Everything seemed very impersonal. Jonathon pulled himself up on edge at yet another although temporarily welcome venue. "Yes," he agreed. "This is the place the company organized for me in Cape Town."

The man looked curiously at Jonathon. He had not been informed why he and his co-driver had been told to bring the young man here from the hospital only that there had been a long car journey from the Namibian coast.

Jonathon held the plastic container the nurse had given him close to his chest and turned to enter the boarding house. He wondered if the housekeeper was expecting him. Hopefully there would be something for him to eat. Nervously he knocked at the front door. After no immediate response he knocked again more urgently. He was alone but for the housekeeper inside. Then he heard footsteps approaching and the blowsy middle-aged woman appeared at the half open door.

"Hullo," she said. Jonathon was becoming more and more uneasy and paranoid in the situation. He felt like a naughty boy. Did this woman also know about his exploits and all that had ensued?

"Kom binne." She gestured him inside. She gave no hint of expecting him but as it seemed to the young man she was looking at him little maliciously. He grabbed at the thought that it was only because her household duties in the boarding house had been unexpectedly upset. She continued:

"I will give you supper."

Jonathon was relieved at this. He still held the plastic box containing the rough diamond gem. He ventured:

"May I use the telephone please?"

She shrugged. He took this to mean her assent.

Jonathon remembered where the telephone was in the boarding house. Suddenly the urgency of the situation came home to him He must speak to Marijke. She would have some mature understanding about what had happened. He must contact her. He heard a footfall as he picked up the receiver. Was the housekeeper waiting to know why he was here at this time of the evening when she had not been expecting him?

The footsteps faded then he lost track of them while he concentrated on dialing Marijke's number. He tried to look over his shoulder while waiting for Marijke to answer and thought that he saw the edge of her dress while she might have been passing down the passage. Was it his imagination? Then he heard a controlled female voice on the other end of the line.

"Who is it?" Jonathon told her it was he. She was clearly startled. She raised her voice

"Jonathon why are you 'phoning? And at this time? You said that you would only be back in six weeks time. What has happened?"

Jonathon answered keeping his voice to the loudest whisper he could manage. He tried to hear whether the housekeeper was within earshot with his other ear. He did not want gossip spreading around the boarding house. He began to speak:

"Marijke I must see you. Can you come round soon this evening? I have had the most terrifying experiences." He looked round to see if the housekeeper was in sight. Then he continued:

"It is to do with my job. I am speaking from Cape Town at the boarding house. I need your help in getting home to the United Kingdom. Marijke's studied but clipped voice came over the line:

"You can't talk now it seems. I will leave right away. My flat is quite nearby. I'll see you in half an hour. I am curious to know what has happened."

Jonathon breathed a sigh of relief. Then he tensed again. Would they be heard speaking together after they arrived? Marijke would have to know why he needed to leave. But he felt her to be a possible confidante in what was happening. He would tell her everything. Slyly because he did not want to start a conversation with the sulky old housemother he coaxed a sandwich of out her and also a cup of coffee. Silently she prepared this for Jonathon.

He took the repast and then heard a car drawing outside the old boarding house in the quiet residential area. He put down his supper on the little commode by the bed and went to greet Marijke. She was just getting out of her car when he opened the front door. Irritatingly the housekeeper came up behind him wanting to know who it was. Jonathon not wishing her to know anything about what was going on regarding his and Marijke's presence at the boardinghouse turned and said to her:

"It's just a friend of mine. I was expecting her."

The old woman still hovered in the doorway as Jonathon welcomed Marijke who began by saying with a slight frown:

"Jonathon, what . . . ." She stopped talking as Jonathon interrupted in a hoarse whisper:

"It's urgent and very secret that I want to talk to you about."

He turned his head and saw the old woman just disappearing down the corridor inside. Marijke answered:

"We'll go inside then to discuss this, your being in Cape Town before these six weeks you were supposed to be working on the diamond barge out at sea are over."

She followed him inside to his room in the boarding house. Fortunately there was a spare chair and Marijke sat down. Jonathon sat on the bed. He could not even speak at first but felt it was vital that she know his predicament. He though it best to take the bull by the horns, so stuttered out the words:

"Marijke I think I am being framed for committing suicide."

Marijke was a tough person so took the confidentiality from Jonathon calmly, and questioned him for the reason for the statement he had just made:

"What happened Jonathon?"

The memory of the last horrific three days made him nearly shake but he began to explain with Marijke listening attentively. Jonathon said to the intent young Dutch girl who had a worried frown on her face. Her friend was nearly shaking she could see at the recollection of some event that he had just experienced. She tried to be patient in the waiting to hear what it was all about. Jonathon managed to gulp out the words:

"I'll tell you the whole story Marijke. It's not a pretty tale." Marijke said:

"Just spell it out slowly then. I am very curious to hear all about it why you are back in Cape Town so soon."

Jonathon was calming slightly. He responded to her cool controlled attitude in what she realized now was some sort of crisis Jonathon was in. But Jonathon's words were muddled. He said:

"They didn't like me, the ship's crewhands that I was working with. And Marijke I had the bad news that my mother has committed suicide. That is what is behind this drama that I am going through."

Marijke gave a start at this news. As is normal in hearing about what was an isolated occurrence such as this, something that happened from time to time, she felt complete horror in knowing about it. She felt helpless to know what to say to her friend. Such events always seemed to point fingers. The deceased person usually had an unreasonable train of though at the time of taking their own life. She said fatuously:

"Why did she do that Jonathon? What caused her action?"

Jonathon humiliated now in having confided just one of the sequence of events that had caused their being together in this conversation answered:

"I don't know exactly. It has something to do with my late grandmother's obsessive nature and her daughter, that was my mother choosing to nurse during the wartime blitz in London."

There was a pause then while the two young people tried to muster an adult steadying in their thinking in this painful act on the part of Jonathon's mother, painful not only to her son but to all who had known her.

Jonathon raised his head with his face taut with tension. He whipped out the words:

"But that's not all Marijke."

Chapter 11

Marijke was already looking afraid at what she was being told but Jonathon continued:

"My ego and ability to do my duty as a supervisor to the crewhands who were doing the heavy work aboard, just plummeted. After what happened to Tasha my mother I no longer felt confident or in control either of myself or of the crew under me.

The ship's captain and officers gave me a nasty feeling because they knew about my mother's death. It came through the ship's radio. They all heard. They gave me little sympathy. And the worst is Marijke it was Tasha herself who said that I should have gone for a land job. She warned me that I would not be able to handle a seaboard occupation and now I feel I'm to blame because of her death."

Marijke pulled herself up in answering:

"It's like that for many people who take their own lives. It causes questions to be asked and blame to be put on those closest to the victim. But nobody ever knows the truth."

Marijke was vaguely feeling her way in giving Jonathon some comfort. She tried to take his mind off the subject by saying:

"So what's the next step Jonathon? Do you even know?"

Jonathon replied with a lowered head:

"I expect a representative of the company will be contacting me by telephone in the morning. I feel very guilty and afraid of the consequences of what I have done." But why," said Marijke. "You have not committed a crime. What else did happen Jonathon? You still seem to have a lot on your mind. I can tell." Jonathon blurted out the words that he had told her before.

"I jumped ship. Into the ocean. They are now framing me for an attempted suicide. The doctor in the hospital after the incident off the Namibian coast told me that ought to see a psychiatrist. But Marijke it was not that. That was not my intention, not at all. You do not know the worst Marijke, the reason why I threw myself overboard"

He stopped, emotion sweeping right through him. Marijke was urgent in her questioning and anxious herself at being, if only in conversation with Jonathon involved in all this. Trembling Jonathon said at his recalling the incident:

"One of the men threatened me. With a knife. That was why I tried to escape. Please Marijke believe me. I was not attempting suicide. I wanted to swim to shore. I just didn't know how impossible that was until I landed in the seawater off the ship."

Their conversation drew to a close as the evening wore one. They were both tiring now especially Jonathon who had come through an emotional day. Marijke said:

"I must go now. Please Jonathon let me know what happens with all this."

Jonathon's memory jerked even at the latish hour that night. He said:

"Oh! Marijke there is just one more thing that I want to tell you about."

He had remembered that he was still in possessions of the little sand encrusted diamond stone that he had kept. He said:

"See here." He felt in his pocket. Marijke was feeling drowsy but started up at what he said before she went on her way, saying curiously:

"What is that?"

He put out his hand for her to see it, with the shining part towards her of the little rough diamond encoated with sea sand of the ocean. He said:

"This is only one of many thousands of stones pulled up by the workers on the diamond mining dredger. The diamond chips are washed down river from the source of the alluvial bearing area inland.

I found it in the pocket of the clothing that I was wearing after I had jumped ship. One of the men must have planted it on me thinking that if it was discovered on my person I would be caught in stealing from the company. But nobody knows." Marijke said:

"If you have to go before the company board of employers about this are you going to keep it to yourself?" Jonathon answered:

"I do not feel guilty about it. No one will ever know if I keep it. It could not possibly be missed."

Marijke taking up her jacket to leave said in answer to his admission about the little gem that he decided to keep and tell no one about, said:

"You are sure to receive a call from the company board to morrow." "Yes," he replied, "I will probably have to go into town and face the music after what has happened."

Climbing into her car on the still warm evening Marijke said:

"Let me know what happens and if I can be of any help."

The next day dawned. Dimly through the heaviness that the night's sleep had left with Jonathon, in the stirrings of the next morning he heard the strident ringing of a telephone somewhere at the far end of the boarding house. Somehow he knew even in those moments with the jarring sound awakening him fully, the tones entering his consciousness as he surfaced from sleep, that this had to do with him. The telephone very seldom rang in the boardinghouse even in the short time that he had resided there.

Yes, he was right. He pulled on his toweling robe from the cupboard that had been left very neatly he noticed in that instant. He was a not that tidy a person. It must have been the motherly though irritating woman who was the housekeeper who had straitened out the mess of clothing. He recalled having left it like that at his departure on the morning after what he now realized only too keenly had been a most unsavory gathering on the other side of the mountain by the sea the night before he had left for duty aboard ship.

He knew now that he had been doped by some sort of narcotics. He heard the grating sound of the housekeeper's voice calling him from some distant part of the boarding house. Jonathon did not even know the way to the place where the telephone stood. Her voice came nearer and nearer to his ears. He tried to raise his own voice in answer to what was now nothing less than an urgent summons to him to take the call.

"Mr. Albany, Mr. Albany are you coming to take this call? There is a very angry person on the other end of the line who wants to speak to you. Are you dressed for the day? You must come and take the call. Now."

At the housekeeper's shout for him Jonathon nearly stumbled over a soliciticiously placed doorstopper at the open door to hurry down the passageway into the hall where the telephone was. The housekeeper was there holding the receiver and saying,

"Yes, he is here. I'll put him on the line right now sir."

"Hullo, Hullo?" Jonathon's slightly upped confidence at receiving the call was soon axed when he heard the sharp sound of the communication from the other end of the line. The other person in the conversation that was about to take place hesitated, but soon came forth with a string of instructions.

"Is that Mr. Jonathon Albany speaking? I need to speak to Mr. Albany urgently." "Yes," answered Jonathon, "this is Mr. Albany here."

The man on the other end said. "I need to make an important appointment for you, Mr. Albany at our offices in the upper part of Cape Town. There has been a serious transgression on your part as far as your employment with this company is concerned. You will have to attend a hearing before the board of directors of the company."

The person went on to state the time of day and address where Jonathon should present himself. Jonathon was practically dumbstruck at the consequences of what he had done, but did try and see in his mind the positive side of the developments this far since evading the tense atmosphere aboard the diamond dredger by jumping ship.

The minutes and hours before the hearing ticked endlessly by as he waited tensely to keep the appointment as the company's representative had asked. He was under no illusions. It was not going to be a pleasant experience. Then it was time to leave for the hearing.

He made sure that the little sand encrusted diamond that he had found on his person was safe in it's box. Somehow for all the sinking of his ego in his personal confidence in this, and also Tasha's suicide, he was determined not to let out anything about the little gem. He consoled himself that it had been a malicious prank on the part of the one of the dredger's crew hands to try and frame him for stealing. He was not a thief. No doubt about it, it had been a war of nerves aboard the mining vessel in which no one was the winner except that it was that he who was quite clearly going to be out of a job after the company hearing was over

Jonathon somehow snapped his thinking together as he came out into the frosty early morning to take the bus to the company headquarters. It would just be an ordeal and then he would be a free man again. Free to leave the country so full of horrors as he was experiencing. His spirits dropped again as he arrived outside the tall impressive building where the hearing would take place.

He stumbled slightly on the front steps taking him into the building. His ego sank again as he saw brassy looking blonde at the reception desk. She glared at him or so it seemed to him. He put his question:

"Is this the right place where my hearing by the board is to take place at 9 a.m. this morning? I am Jonathon Albany. The blonde narrowed her eyes and stared at him as if he were an insect then spoke after some long seconds.

"Yes indeed. The representatives of the company are waiting in the company boardroom for you. She looked him carefully up and down over the top of her spectacles. I will show you the way. Follow me."

Jonathon noticed that she was not being very pleasant in her dealing with him. He went after her and she ushered him fussily through a frighteningly large door. What hit his eyes inside was and imposing looking group older men attired ever so smartly all with grim expressions on their faces. One of them sat at the head of a large polished table around which they all sitting. The man at the head addressed Jonathon grimly. It was quite clear that the chairperson was under no illusions about what had happened. His tone was tight and unfriendly:

"Mr. Jonathon Albany?" Jonathon noticed that he was not being asked to sit down. Obviously this was not going to be one cosy chat. The chairman began the proceedings:

"You are aware, Mr. Albany the you have hugely embarrassed this company by which you are employed?"

Jonathon had not known exactly what to expect in this hearing but did realize that it was going to be unpleasant for him. Thinking as he stood there he felt anger surge into a rush through his body. This was not his fault. No, not for several reasons. Firstly Tasha his mother had caused a nervousness in him that had finally nearly caused him a breakdown by her suicide.

This was one reason. As he stood there isolated because these company representatives clearly had a lot of ill feeling towards him, the other reasons of unfairness flashed into his mind. Meanwhile the members of the company board muttered amongst themselves and shuffled important looking documents.

Jonathon's thoughts were inward as the board prepared for the hearing. The marijuana that had been offered to him? That was not his fault either. The sinking of his ego in the whole situation causing an inability to do his duty on board amongst the diamond mining dredger ship crew? That had only been made worse when he had been threatened with a knife. And it had all come to the point where he had been forced to take the decision to jump overboard.

The chief member of the board cleared his voice as Jonathon's thoughts came to a head. This chairperson looked up and addressed Jonathon.

"We do not want to prolong this hearing. It is equally trying for yourself as well as wasting the company's time."

At these words Jonathon felt like a schoolboy being reprimanded by a headmaster. The person continued.

"I will be straightforward and ask you outright. Was there any particular reason for your jumping ship? We can find no reason or action on the part of our company to have caused you to take this step."

Quickly Jonathon had another thought rush to his head. No he was not going to tell the board about the party where the narcotics had been offered to him. Neither was he going to tell them about the knife attack. Nor about the little sand encrusted diamond stone that had been planted on his person the night before he had jumped overboard. Why should he? The chairman's words were going right over Jonathon's head. He was hardly aware that the man was speaking to him. Then through his subconscious he heard his name in the auditorium.

"Mr. Albany?" Then again. "Mr. Albany? Have you anything to say in response to the proposition that we are putting forward for you?"

The chairperson clearly had the upper hand personally. Jonathon had done wrong it was apparent and was being given the chance to clear his name if he could. The chairman went on:

"Have you anything at all to say in your defence? You have caused the utmost inconvenience in this situation as you must surely realize. Yes our helicopter is kept on standby off the Namibian coast but we do not expect to have to use it. It is fortunate in the saving of your life that the pilot was on duty."

Jonathon raised his head. The chairperson was getting vociferous. Jonathon looked up and tried to summon up the courage to stare the man in the eye and respond with something to say for his own protection but he could not. Just a croaking mumble of words came out of his mouth.

"Yes sir of course I realize that I did wrong. But sir my family circumstances were adrift."

The chairperson was quite ready to stamp out any kind of response from this young man who had caused an infinite lot of trouble for the company in fact the very worst that could have been expected, and said:

"Your family circumstances have nothing to do with what has happened."

The aggressive male forwardness of the chairperson made Jonathon who was after all male himself, have a rise of blood to his face. Tasha, poor Tasha could not come to his help now. No. She was dead. And she would have given this arrogant man such a piece of her mind. So he cleared his voice and spoke:

"If you will understand sir, it was the recent suicide of my mother, the shock of it that cause me to lose control in the supervision of the men on board." Not for anything was Jonathon going to let on about the knife threat aboard, and the little sea diamond. The circumstances were bad enough as it was.

Suddenly Jonathon felt very alone and up against these men with no one to support his cause. This was not even his country. He began to think at a rapid pace panicking now, in the only way he knew as an adult. That was as a student. He began to question and find some sort of reason and logic in what he was enduring. Surely these grimfaced and unfriendly people could do nothing to harm him? It was clear that they were out to express the dissatisfaction and inconvenience of the company with Jonathon, a former senior ranking member of the diamond mining barge anchored off the Orange River mouth.

Jonathon thought quickly into the reality of the situation and plucked courage at a break in the tirade of disapproval coming his way by saying as clearly as he could:

"I realize that I have not fulfilled my obligations to the company by my act. I must make it clear that it was not a suicidal act. I will accept notice of resignation from the company for this."

Jonathon's words just seemed to float in the air but they caused an irritated outburst of words from the chairperson:

"I am afraid my young man that the company does not accept that statement. It was quite clear to the officer on watch on the day you jumped ship that was your intention. What else did you think your were going to achieve by taking that action? I am afraid we cannot accept what you are saying. According to our employment section you had the mental capacity when you were taken on to hold down the job no matter what happened. This has proved erroneous and you will have to leave. The interview is now terminated.

A last stipulation from the board is that you consult a psychiatrist. We think you need to do this in a final act on the company's part to clear its name and see that its employee suffered no harm from any act of theirs. We will post you a letter of termination of service and an address of a psychiatrist that we want you to consult."

Jonathon did not even try to state the fact that it had originally been his attention to swim ashore. That would only mean more involvement in the present scene, especially that he did not at this present time want to mention anything about the knife attack he had experienced on board. Nor about the party where he had been offered the marijuana that had affected his mind for some days following aboard ship.

There were a few moments of near quiet with only the sound of the members legs and feet shuffling under the large polished board room table and the rustling sound of the official papers being put together before them. Then harshly again came the chairperson's words to Jonathon's ears:

"You are being suspended from service as from a month from today. We are within our rights to expect a psychiatrist's report within a month. We have asked Dr. Thorne to let us have this information as soon as he is satisfied with the situation as far as you apparent suicide is concerned."

Jonathon opened his mouth wishing that he could hotly deny this accusation. This man showed no sympathy and was not mincing his words. Little did he know the truth and Jonathon was saying no more about what had actually happened to cause what the board had against him. No he would save what else he had to say for the psychiatrist's ears. He was a medical doctor too as Jonathon was quick to realize because of his late mother's nursing involvements. He knew he need not be afraid although he thought to himself that he had never expected it would come to this. Again the chairperson's words came to his ears.

"Hearing adjourned." Addressing the young man he said: "You may leave the meeting now."

Slowly Jonathon turned to go. All his hopes and excitement at working with a diamond mining company just crumbled into the pathetic figure who was slowly walking out into what was at least, for this time of the year in Cape Town, the never changing warm fresh air of the outside.

He felt at a complete loss. His board and lodging was paid for a month. He supposed that he would have a series of appointments with the psychiatrist. No he had never thought it would come down to this. He waited at the bus stop and was back in the boarding house now just a place to be in this strange land, that was very temporary in his life.

He snapped out of his daze. Life must go on. He must telephone Marijke to tell her the worst about his failure and that he would have to get back to Great Britain by the end of the next thirty days. He also had another call to make yes, to the psychiatrist, Dr. Thorne. He could not breathe a sigh of relief just yet.

Jonathon sat in the little room on the bed in the boarding house that morning wondering if the telephone was free for use. The only way would be to get up and walk down the passage to see. He found Marijke's number and took the number of the psychiatrist that he had been given at the hearing the day before and made his way hopefully to the telephone stand.

The hall was empty but he realized that anyone could walk by and hear the very personal nature of the two calls he knew that he had to make. He put the numbers written down on the space next to the very out of date telephone receiver. He dialed Marijke's number hoping that because it was a Saturday she would not be involved with her studies. He was too right. He immediately recognized her voice:

"Hullo? Hullo? Who is it?" Jonathon made his communication clear. "Marijke, Marijke, please listen. It's Jonathon Albany. I am in a very bad state. I have had to give up my job. I would like you to help me book a passage by air back to Great Britain. If you can get here to the old boarding house where you know that I am staying I would be grateful."

Then he thought he had better let her know a little of why he was seeking her help. He lowered his voice for fear of being heard.

"Marijke my mother has committed suicide. She took her own life just over a week ago. I thought you should know. She liked your family you see."

The telephone mouthpiece crackled over the air with age and frequent use. Then Marijke's voice came over the line:

"I don't believe it Jonathon but I will see you shortly after lunch. I can't talk now." Jonathon knew she would help because of her typical Dutch nature of putting matters right even if only temporarily. Yes thought Jonathon, just like the Hollanders. That was one urgent call over. He began to feel more cheerful. Now for the psychiatrist. His heart dropped again. What he had to do he knew he must, was make an appointment with Dr. Thorne as he had been asked to by the Chairman of the Board at the hearing. He gingerly picked up the telephone again dialed the number he had been given.

Jonathon felt an eerie sensation down his spine. Marijke had been with him briefly after lunch at the boarding house. She was not impressed he could tell by what Jonathon had to say about his ordeal. She left irritated that she would have to arrange his departure back to Great Britain. Jonathon spent the rest of the weekend sleeping off both the experience aboard ship and the nasty feeling left in him of the hearing afterwards by the company board of directors.

Monday came around then and Jonathon was up early to prepare for his appointment with the psychiatrist Dr. Thorne. At first he felt good about this but when he found himself speaking to the receptionist he began to feel shivers go up and down his spine. The horrors of paranoia that he had experienced after the knife threat incident aboard the diamond dredger tingled in his brain.

Did the woman know something about what had happened? She seemed to be expecting him to call but did not actually say so. A creeping sense of his imagination going out of control swept over him. Was this what the marijuana had done to him? And to make the brittle situation worse was Tasha's death, yes her suicide making it even less bearable?

Then he thought doctors and especially psychiatrists were used to things like this. Surely the receptionist did not know the bare facts of his predicament. Her words were like icicles penetrating his brain, at least that is what he felt like. Then he heard his name called:

"Mr. Albany we can give you a cancelled appointment this afternoon. Dr. Thorne is free at two thirty. Our rooms are in the area that you are staying in."

How did she know that, Jonathon pondered briefly. The receptionist must be getting on in years to know the suburb so well as to be able to give him directions as she was doing.

"Yes, up Durant Street just as you walk up the road from your boarding house. Then it's the third road to the right. I will give you our address then you will have no trouble finding it." Jonathon answered:

"Thank you, I will be there in good time this afternoon, just as soon as I have had lunch."

Clearly this appointment with Dr. Thorne the psychiatrist was going to be quite unpleasant given the circumstances that he was going to have to explain to the doctor. Then subdued as he finally sat in the patient's chair facing the pschyciatrist Jonathon said:

"Good morning doctor." There was no immediate response. Clearly this was not going to be some affable chitchat between he and Dr. Thorne for the next half hour. The doctor put his fingertips together and pursed his lips. Just the doctor's slight movement made Jonathon feel even worse than when he had walked into the man's consulting room. Nervously he waited for the doctor to say something to break the ice. Then to Jonathon's near paranoid state the Doctor's words entered into his consciousness:

"Did you attempt suicide Jonathon?"

A paranoid feeling burned inside him. How did the Doctor know the situation? How did the Doctor know the situation? How could he in his now cowed state tell the Doctor step by step what had actually happened. He kept mum. It was surely a questioning role that this Doctor must play. Jonathon felt right then that he did not want to confide anything in this man who had now put on a pair of spectacles.

Clearly he was taking a good look at Jonathon's demeanour. He suddenly spoke sharply:

"Jonathon!" The doctor was obviously trying to communicate with him get through to him. "Jonathon why did you try to take your own life. The company knows you did this."

Jonathon gasped. Was this what they were holding against him? He stuttered out some words, garbled because he felt completely overcome by the Doctor's assumption of what had happened. Weakly Jonathon replied further:

"I just wanted to swim . . . ." He could get nothing more out of his mouth. It seemed that his tongue was tied. The Doctor, seeming out to prove and cause Jonathon to accept that the action of the young man was suicide, was working on his mind to such a way as to make the young man believe something that was quite untrue. The Doctor was about twenty years his senior in age so it was easy for the older man to take the upper hand in the tète á tète. So Jonathon's words were all he could muster up at first. He was denying what the doctor was suggesting:

"No not at all." His words reverberated in his mind. Was the effect of the marijuana still with him?

The interview finished on a subdued note for Jonathon. This doctor with his accusing and sharp questioning was clearly trying to pin him down according to the wishes of his company employers. The company were firmly of the opinion that Jonathon's action was a case of suicide. The director of the company, to justify the irregularity of what had happened and the inconvenience to all concerned, was wanting to have a complete report justifying Jonathon's action of jumping overboard. During the consultation he tried to put the young man in a situation where he would be forced to admit this.

The psychiatrist was becoming irritated by Jonathon's stubborn attitude in the following consultation of his taking his own life by drowning. Jonathon could see that he would have to prove the mental strength he had found in himself both now and aboard ship, and what had occurred in between.

After the psychiatrist's accusation he felt challenged to confide in Dr. Thorne about the marijuana party and the threat with the crew member's knife at his throat as a result. Perhaps the Doctor would understand then that these two connected occurrences had been the cause of what Jonathon found it in himself to insist on the fact that he must dare to disagree that the "man overboard' drama had a provocation for this. So Jonathon spoke to the Doctor:

"I was scared at the time of the knife threat. If I had acted aggressively then it could have been fatal. The threat was interrupted by the arrival of the Captain of the ship and the officers. But I could not tolerate the tension aboard fearing it might happen again, with the sinking of my ego in my situation. This was because of hearing of my mother's own death recently by suicide. I heard the news while I was in the mining operations in Sierra Leone. I was handling my rank hopelessly because of this.

So you see Doctor I was forced into this. I must insist though that I had no intention of suicide. It was just bad judgment on my part in thinking that I could swim to shore. Then the helicopter rescued me from drowning." Affirmatively Jonathon got up to leave quite angry at the doctor's manipulation.

Chapter 12

He suddenly felt that he had come out of a phase in his maturing that excluded Jean and his mother. This Dutch girl had been such a support to him in this ordeal that he had come through, something that for all the psychiatrist's questioning and probing he would always have as part of his life. Suddenly it hit him. Marijke was the one for him.

He thought in agreement of Tasha's suggestion that they become closely acquainted that this was an opportunity for a partner. Jean still pulled at his heartstrings but somehow that was all over. There was no work in England for someone of his qualifications. Marijke's father worked on the gold mines in Johannesburg. They had already been introduced and he knew Tasha had put in a persuasive word regarding a land based engineering job for him.

Marijke as they walked on the sandy beach in the warm Cape morning felt very close to Jonathon. She knew so much about him now and her Dutch practicality and knowledge of South Africa were to Jonathon's advantage in what could be a new life.

Without Jean? Suddenly she was far away from his present thoughts.

Now he was out of the psychiatrist's clutches he thought. It was Tasha who had instigated the whole thing and his father who had put him up to going to sea, something to do with his own experiences in the wartime aboard the aircraft carrier that he had wanted his son to follow in his footsteps. Then he spoke to Marijke:

"Shall we go back for some coffee at the boarding house? Marijke answered: "That will be wonderful Jonathon. We have had quite some socializing here in Cape Town, almost an adventure together. Although you have had the most exciting part." Jonathon answered:

"I must say I did not want to get involved with those smokers at the party those few nights ago. They caught me for a sucker those Afrikaners. That drug habit is something that has reached South Africa from America after the horrors of the Vietnam war. The whole drug culture with the general political situation in the world has just seeped into this society here."

They walked together a little further along the beach pensive about what Jonathon had involved himself in with the events that had taken place after making the mistake of falling for a marijuana cigarette. Needing to communicate at this thought Jonathon spoke, the gusts of wind typical of the Cape at this time of year nearly blowing his words away.

"Marijke do you think Dirk at the party last week meant to do me harm? It has turned out alright yes, with me being safe but there could have been a very nasty and tragic end to the whole episode in my life. And Marijke no one would have known why if I had met my death by drowning."

Marijke turned her face to the sea and took a deep breath against the wind that was whipping up sand as they made their way to her car.

"No Jonathon. The action of offering a marijuana cigarette was meant in kindness though in a very underhand way. Dirk didn't know what the consequences would be. It was meant to calm and soothe you take your mind off the present at the time. He and his friends were experiencing extreme tension at the political clamp down and you seeming just like one of he and his friends he thought he was doing you a favor. It's over now anyway."

Jonathon looked relieved at what she had just said. What a thoughtful person, he surmised. Suddenly he remembered something. The little sea sand encrusted diamond that had been planted on him during the night before he had jumped ship. Where was it? Then he realized that he was wearing the same clothes as those that he had worn when he had left the little hospital in the desert off the mining barge. He had not had time to have them laundered.

Frantically he felt in his pocket. He had told no one about it neither at the company hearing nor the psychiatrist at the necessary following consultation. He felt urgently in his pocket. At this action Marijke looked at him curiously. He was an intriguing person. She said:

"What are you looking for Jonathon?" "It's this. It's this," he said his hands shaking as he felt the little stone pressing into his body. They both stopped in the blowing sand with the sea churning in the south easter wind in the distance behind him as the day drew on.

Jonathon surprised himself to find the little stone that his whole life was revolving around now. He had not forgotten about it permanently and now wanted to tell someone about his aquiring the little stone. It seemed to cast a good omen on their relationship that was working into a closeness between the two young people.

As he stood there he thought: Jean! Yes, Jean. She would never have understood what he had been through and why. She did not know South Africa. Marijke did. Somehow he felt that now both Jean and Tasha, poor dead Tasha, who had been his mother, stood for everything that was weak in a female. Because of what he had come through in this whole episode in his life he needed someone who knew South Africa and South Africans, like Marilize and Petronella for all their trying to get the better of one another in their sharp but friendly jibes at one another. Marijke always looked on benignly though as Jonathon could tell it was always amicable.

Jonathon said:

"Let's go back for coffee now. I want to confide in you Marijke what actually happened after the party that night in the seaside bungalow that night, in the little cottage on the seafront."

Then with steaming mugs of coffee to end the day and to warm them during the cool of the mid evening Jonathon began. The aroma from the hot sweet coffee hit his nostrils for a few moments coming to him pleasantly and he said:

"Is marijuana addictive Marijke? Do you know?" "All that I know,' she said is that it takes you out of yourself in stressful times. It can make you sick too."

"Well," said Jonathon, the coffee cooling to a drinkable temperature, "this is a lesson to me because it was having its effect on me right until a calamity happened. Yes you do know about about my mother's suicide? I thought I told you." "Yes?" she answered giving a little start at hearing this news, perhaps again. Her parents had liked Jonathon's family. He continued:

"What happened was that I was given a hearing by the company because I was rescued from throwing myself into the ocean from the diamond dredger that I was working on out at sea off the Orange river mouth." Marijke was astounded:

"You fell overboard?" He said tersely: "No Marijke. I did it on purpose. I jumped overboard." Marijke was a young woman who kept up her poise and self control. She had grown to like Jonathon greatly in a very short time as Tasha had known she would. Marijke was now slightly alarmed at this confidence in her for it was clear that he needed to speak about his experience. She gathered her thoughts together and a little sharply in the tension of the moment enquired:

"Why Jonathon, why did you do that?"

Immediately if somewhat desperately Jonathon fell for the interest she was showing. She was clearly prepared to be a supportive confidante in what he had to tell her. He tried to reach out to Marijke verbally after they had driven back to the boarding house. They sat in Jonathon's room in the residence on the faded but comfortable chairs. Jonathon had managed to rustle up two more cups of steaming coffee from the kitchen for them both. Marijke ever alert said:

"I know you well now Jonathon. There must have been a very good reason for risking your life."

Jonathon wanted to pour out to her what had happened in truth:

"You see the problem is my family particularly my mother who as you know has taken her own life. I had to have two sessions with the psychiatrist here in Cape Town at the company's request. These interludes, and talking the whole situation out as it involves me at present made me realize that my whole status and ego was crumbling within me. I could not keep up the superior rank with all its duties that I had been given. I only just tolerated the teasing and bonhomie from the manual workers aboard the diamond mining dredger I was billoted on. In the end I could not take their attitude towards me and I became aggressive. I am not normally like this. I was threatened by one of the workers at knifepoint as a result.

Suddenly the whole atmosphere aboard became tense and intolerable for me. I made a plan to swim ashore but when I actually did this as I told you I found myself in the ice cold sea swelling up and down with huge waves. My scheme to get to shore became hopeless. The Officer on watch summoned the helicopter on guard on land that flew in to help and fortunately, very fortunately they saved my life. All I have to show for the adventure is the little sea diamond that was planted on me hoping that I would be incriminated in revenge by my enemies on board."

Marijke pretended not to be as concerned as she really was. She felt ever more strongly about this young man who was asking in so many words to be understood, for some support in what he had done, to solve the problem that he had created for himself. As she thought her reaction to what he had told her came to her. No! No! This was not his fault. Not at all. It needed deeper questioning and understanding especially by her.

She was the one he was focusing on. Then she thought quickly at the sight of his despairing face. She spoke waiting for the mug of coffee to cool to a drinkable temperature.

"Jonathon." She had his attention. Her sharp but at the same time mellow and comforting voice pulled him up. He needed a woman's discipline even after those two appointments with the psychiatrist. He looked up hopefully. Marijke saw that she had the dominance in the situation so spoke carefully not wanting to hurt him any more than he was at the moment.

"Jonathon you tell me that your mother committed suicide. Now I find that most distressing both for myself and for you."

Jonathon frowned worriedly. He was trying still not to think about this hard fact that Marijke had brought up. The doctor had advised such an attitude by him. He replied:

"Yes Marikje I agree." "Why was this?" She queried determinedly. "It was a mess her whole life," Jonathon answered. "She was trying to help in London when the city was being attacked by Nazi bombers. She was very brave but I think personally the reality of what she and her co-nurses had done during that time only hit home to her more and more severely as she grew older and tried to keep her family going.

She did a lot for her parents but was particularly bothered by her mother, Alice who was my grandmother. This old person was someone who lived in what I can only say was a sort of fantasy world. Yes my grandparents were quite wealthy with the old family Great House as it was called.

My grandfather was sensible enough but it amused him that Alice his wife used to go ferreting around in curio shops and junk shops and boutiques ever searching for what she was certain that she was going to find eventually, that priceless item of art forgotten for centuries but found by her. All this was to please my grandfather whom she doted on.

Marijke said:

"Your mother seems to have been the problem in your life. I do know that the male gender are always very attached to their female parent. This seems to me to be the root of what has happened to you right through the generations in your family." "Yes," said Jonathon, "Tasha did not even like my girl friend that I had while a student." Marijke he could see was looking curious at this last statement. Was she jealous? Was he imagining that?

Her strength of mind and character contrasting with in his own situation which had weakened him in his personal life impressed him. Somehow as they sat together Marijke seemed to control the circumstances they were in. This was understood when his thoughts were jarred in the silence. She said. "I will have to book your 'plane ticket back to Great Britain, you asked me to." Suddenly Jonathon did not want to be without her support in his life. Tasha had even said while she was alive that Marijke's parents could help him find employment in gold mining.

Jean and the United Kingdom were very far away. Impulsively in a weak moment he broke out, "Book two tickets Marijke. One for you and one for me." She replied startled at these unexpected words: "That's not what I was thinking. Is this to do with you and your family in England?"

Jonathon who had turned away reflectively from the svelte young girl for a moment now faced her and stated undeniably as he knew they both felt, even physically.

"You will have a lot to do with my family Marijke. I want to marry you and come back to South Africa with you. I want to introduce you to my father and especially, my dear old grandfather Grant. He has only got one or more two years to live and he and I get on very well. I know he has a soft spot for me and would like me to be happy after all the chiding I have had from Tasha."

Then again immediately he remembered Jean. Sweet Jean. But she was no longer part of his life and could never be anymore. She would now be part of all that was in the past when he took on a land based job of work here in South Africa. As Jonathon had noticed about Marijke and her self control, in the current moments she did not bat an eyelid.

She did lowered her head a little and gave out no words of acceptance at first to Jonathon's offer. His heart thumped inside him. Then she spoke:

"But what will we do for and engagement ring Jonathon?"

Jonathon now knew this was her acceptance of his proposal. Wildly at these words of hers he responded:

"The sea diamond! The sea diamond that I showed you! I will have it cut and polished and set into a ring clasp for you Marijke. Slowly but covertly she smiled to herself. She had made a catch. Then his spirits sank slightly again. Wouldn't Grant want him to have his grandmother Alice's heirloom engagement for Marijke?

"But of course Jonathon. It will add a little spice to our relationship and be a reminder of my and your time together in Cape Town and when we return to the goldfields. Of course my parents will help you find a mining job up north as it is called here in Cape Town." Jonathon responded:

"Now what we are waiting for is to get onto the 'plane to travel to England so I can introduce you to what's left of my family. I will send a note to Jean my ex girl friend that I am engaged. Although I was very fond of her she was never a feature in my life who gave me back up and inspiration like you do. This I have found in you Marijke, a constant lift to my spirits. Your constant understanding of my psychological downswing was so supportive and indispensable.

That is mostly over now with the psychiatric treatment. That whole drama aboard the "Agulhas" was caused when I jumped ship. I now accept that it was not an attention seeking suicide as the company board accused me of. Though in appearance it must have seemed that I was trying to end my life by drowning.

It was more than that as I managed to convince the psychiatrist. I do feel better about the whole event now" Marijke said, ever alert: "Yes. We are nearly there. The airhostess is calling for seatbelts. We must have reached landing time at Heathrow airport."

Once they had descended the flight of steps onto the tarmac it was not far to take the train back to Devon and the Great House that would be somewhere to stay while visiting Grant, Jonathon's grandfather. On the way down Jonathon told Marijke a little more about his grandparents.

"Most of the items of Alice's extensive set of collectibles have been sent to the local museum when

Grant left for the rest house for the aged as he had said was his plan. My grandfather wanted my fiancée to have Alice's, that was his wife's engagement ring Marijke."

Jonathon added in passing to Marijke that there would be a catalogue numbering the various collectibles Alice had acquired at the local museum. There he would enquire as to the rose tinted silver filigreed glass box which contained Alice's heirloom ring.

The following day the couple walked down to the old rest home outside the village. On being greeted by one of the carers they were warned that Grant Godiver was not too well at all. He had taken Tasha's death badly and had become ever increasingly poorly in his health. Jonathon was warned to keep his visit a very quiet one because the doctor was expecting Grant's heart to give in at any time.

The old gentleman was terribly distressed over his daughter's taking her own life. As he lay there knowing that his much doted on grandson was waiting to see him with his fiancée his heart quickened. He could not understand in his close on senility why Jonathon had a different girlfriend now. Before he had left for South Africa his girlfriend had been Jean wasn't that right? Was this some foreign upstart who had captured Jonathon's fancy? And he had been told she was his fiancée, the more's too it! The couple were ushered into Grant's sick bay. Typical of old people the old man at first felt perplexed and then completely at a loss. Then he gruffly let out the words:

"So this is your young fiancée? Not Jean?" "No Grandfather," answered Jonathon, "Jean would never leave England and her family here to go to South Africa. I need a wife and Marijke is Dutch and her family are already in South Africa. I am going there with her to take a job of work on the gold mines in Johannesburg. Much better than the other mining occupation at sea."

The old man havered and like all old people Grant put a stubborn front. Hadn't Jonathon been very fond of Jean his student acquaintance? Wasn't this a bit hard on the Scottish lass? But he thought with a sigh, times change and people do too. Jonathon would need strong support from a woman out in the wilds of Africa. The couple would need one another and yes, they seemed very much in love. As Grant grew weaker with their visit he said as his grandson had expected:

"I want you to have Alice's, that is my late wife's engagement ring. It is catalogued and lodged in the local museum here together with all Alice's other acquisitions. I will give you the code number."

The couple took their leave at the end of their visit all the more mature in their young lives at seeing yet another person of Jonathon's family and much loved by him, so sick and nearly at the end of his life. The carer began fussing around the old man because she could see that he was becoming agitated with the visit by his son. It was a family scene and she didn't want the old man to dwell on the upsetting fact of his daughter's suicide.

As it was Grant was showing signs of being disturbed by the presence of Marijke who was apparently new to the family situation. Jonathon and Marijke took their leave. As they came out into the brisk fresh air Jonathon said:

"We might as well go straight to the museum now. I know where it is from going there in childhood days when my grandmother used to take the overflow of her collectibles to the museum to be stored or put on display."

Jonathon led the way. The museum was fortunately open for visitors. Marijke said:

"You do have the catalogue with the code number of the glass silver filigreed container with you? The one you told me about that contains your late grandmother's engagement ring?"

Jonathon replied in the affirmative.

The entered an old door to find a wizened and aged man seated at a desk in an anteroom. The desk was covered with documents, some yellowed with age. The documents Jonathon noticed all had catalogue numbers heading descriptions of the items presumably stored in the museum. Jonathon was interested and curious about what the old man occupied himself with in the work he did in the old display exhibition rooms in the building. He broke the ice at old man's propriety attitude of running the museum while he shuffled the old papers he was working with:

"May I ask what your name is sir?" Jonathon though he ought to show some respect at the old man's obvious conscientious handling of his work day, even though he could see that the museum's curator was a little pompous in his attitude to the newcomers. The old man looked over his bifocal spectacles and answered:

"Mr. Theobald to you sir." Jonathon took this information in silently. "What is your query here today sir?" Jonathon then answered:

"I have the catalogue number of a small silver filigreed cut glass box with a velvet lining that contains my late grandmother's engagement ring. It is a diamond in a clasp."

Mr. Theobald looked a little nervous and put out. He said: "Just give me the catalogue code number, give me the catalogue number. You have it with you? I vaguely remember about this item. It was a ring contained in a false bottom of a rose tinted glass container was it not? Of suberb attractiveness, yes. The item is being stored here at Mr. Grant Godiver's request. You can come with me to see where it is. The catalogue number will help us to locate it."

His voice was quavering as he spoke. It was an untimely interruption to his finishing off of his morning's work satisfactorily. He was obviously a perfectionist in what he did. As the three of them had walked down a long slightly dusty passage they came to the end where the museum displays behind glass cases were on show. Even though the rooms had a musty atmosphere about them there was a faint odor of preservative chemicals used to keep the items on display from disintegrating.

The old man was humming and muttering to himself. He was quite an age that Jonathon and Marijke could tell but the museum was obviously his life long passion. His muttering to himself became the words directed more towards the visiting couple. For a moment he wondered why they were here. He said:

"Now it's the room at the end to the left where old Mr. Godiver's wife's precious articles are on display."

Then he began to reminise:

"The old lady used to come her with artifacts that her husband Mr. Godiver did not like or that they had no room for at the Great House. Several of the many pictures that she brought here I have just stacked in that corner so that anyone interested in art and artists can just flip through them. Most of those are of local appeal."

The old man was rambling on it being obviously a pleasure to him that someone was curious about his museum. He was digressing though and Jonathon with his patience being tried somewhat interrupted:

"Yes, yes. Most fascinating." He thought he had better pander to the old fellow otherwise they would never get away. He spoke interrupting a flow of volubility at a picture by a local artist that had recently been stored at the museum:

"Yes Mr. Theobald. But we have come to locate and claim Mr. Grant Godiver's heirloom ring that is stored in a rose tinted glass holder. Do you understand? This is the reason for our coming here." Jonathon gave Marijke an exasperated look but the old curator broke in speaking irritably:

"Yes. Yes, in here. I know precisely where it is to be found. You have the antique item's catalogue number please?"

The old man took a while to absorb the fact that these folk were at the museum for a specific purpose. He thought regretfully that the governors of the museum, his passion in life had warned that he ought to retire. His showing off of the antique silver, some old vases of Meissen pottery and brass accoutrements of yester year, turned into a waning of his enthusiasm as Jonathon's demeanor became icier and icier as time was being wasted as far as he was concerned. He intimated to the old curator the purpose of his visit, to fetch his late grandmother's heirloom ring in the glass box. The old man seeing his fault was quick to respond:

"Of course, of course. You are wanting the rose tinted cut glass canister. I know exactly where I can lay my hand on the item. Right here."

He pounced on a key lying in a stinkwood box and quickly unlocked an Elizabethan glass fronted cabinet holding besides the rose tinted container that Jonathon recognized immediately, some brass candle holders and china ornamental figures of historical value. They all looked very old antiques and would have been quite valuable to a collector like Alice, Grant's late wife.

The curator's claw like fingers reached into the cabinet and carefully he took out the little container that Jonathon was requiring at his grandfather Grant's request. Pursing his lips at the success of his search the old man almost spat out the words:

"You have the cataloguer number on the receipt?" "Yes," answered Jonathon a little irritated at the delay in finding the item because of the curator's seemingly endless conversation: "Yes. Yes," went on the old man turning the box upside down holding on to the lid as he did so. The number on the base coincides with the one on the receipt that you gave. This is the item you want. Are you taking it away with you? For a small deposit you can take it but it must be returned. That was Mr. Godiver's instruction as I recall when it found its way here." Jonathon spoke in answer:

"We do not want to take it, no. Just the diamond ring that it contains. Mr. Godiver my grandfather has bequeathed it to my fiancée to be." At this the old man was full of smiles.

On hearing this sad news the old curator fumbled a little perturbed. He tried to release the spring that opened the cavity at the bottom of the glass canister. As Grant had shown Jonathon soon after Alice had died the rose tinted cut glass container had a false bottom to keep the diamond ring safe.

There was a velvet lining inside the cask. The curator gently and carefully with little flip now emptied the content onto the dark hued stinkwood cabinet. What a shock they all had when only the clasp of the ring but no diamond fell out. The old man went into a tirade of spluttering and said anxiously:

"The diamond disappeared. I will immediately call my young assistant to see if he knows anything about this."

He went to the side of the room and pressed a button to summon the lackey who did the cleaning of the stored articles in the museum. The youth stuttered in fright and disbelief.

Nothing like this had ever happened before.

The curator briefly questioned him as to when he had seen the ring in its complete state last. The museum assistant muttered:

"Just two or three days ago sir." The curator said in abject tones to Jonathon:

"It has either been lost or stolen. We will make a thorough search for it and let you take the clasp." Jonathon said to Marijke:

"This will be the death of my old grandfather. But I have a plan. From what I recall about my acquisition, shall we call it that from the diamond dredger, that was planted on me—remember I told you how I found it in my pocket after I jumped ship, well I have the sand encoated gem still.

These two diamonds can replace one another, the lost one can be replaced by the sea sand encrusted one. Of course this one of mine, the one that was used in an attempt to incriminate me, that as you know I kept quiet about, I'll have cut and polished to size and set in the original clasp. No one will know the difference. Then when we show it to Grant my grandfather, perhaps it will give him a new lease of life. He would have been very distressed to know that the original diamond belonging to Alice had been lost or stolen. Marijke, it will always remind me about how my life was saved."

At long last the couple were able to get away from the museum. Jonathon said intimately:

"It is going to be a sad feeling that I will have to present my newly engaged fiancée to my dear old grandfather wearing a diamond ring bearing a gem that was not what the old man really wanted. I am on tenterhooks that he will not recognize the other diamond set in the ring, the sea diamond. We'll go straight to the jeweller now so that we can show the finished article to my grandfather soon. He will be the first one to see it on your finger." Marijke swelled with the thrill of it all. Jonathon went on:

"I am sure Alice my grandmother would have approved of what will be put together the clasp with the sea diamond in it. The jeweler will sand the ocean encrustations off the precious stone. This ring Marijke will symbolize all that has happened in our courting. It was not a long one just long enough to be sure of what we are doing.

Jean my student girlfriend took the breakup of our frienship badly, I wrote a letter to her but know that this is what I want. Yes, you Marijke. I did feel a bit of a casanova about my two relationships but there was very little that was physical in Jean and my very shallow attachment. We have seen life you and I, Marijke and you have been a constant support something I want for our future. I told my father over the telephone last night.

Even though he is still in a state of shock over Tasha my mother's suicide he took our news philosophically. We will be lodging at our family home the Great House for a few days until the ring is ready. You will love the place."

A few days later the couple rose early to fetch the heirloom ring with the sea diamond sparkling in the sunlight like the ocean it had been taken up from. The ring was duly put on Marijke's finger and then the couple walked arm in arm over the town to the rest home at the other side where it was quieter.

A nurse greeted them and they were ushered into Grant's presence. Immediately the old man noticed the newly set ring. He looked at it suspiciously as Marijke held out her hand gracefully. Jonathon held his breath. Grant said:

"That's not Tasha's ring is it?"

Jonathon did not want to tell of the mysterious disappearance of the genuine gem for fear of upsetting the old man whom he could see was disbelieving of it so he smoothed over the awkward moment amongst the three of them and just said:

"This is the ring that Marijke and I are betrothed with."

Grant took one more look at the ring and at peace with Jonathon's assurance sank back into his commodious armchair.